THE SECRET OF THE RUNAWAY SERVANTS

THE LIBERTY LADS

BOOK I

GEOFF BAGGETT

ISBN-13: 978-1-946896-05-6

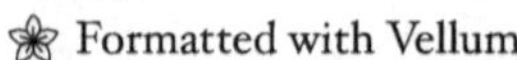
Formatted with Vellum

For all lovers of mystery <u>and</u> history.

Cover Design by Geoff Baggett

A LIBERTY LADS MYSTERY

❧ I ❧
FUGITIVES

March 29, 1775 - Northern Virginia

The dense woods were black as pitch. The two brothers stumbled forward blindly, all the while hoping that they would not fall into a hole, creek, gully, or pond. Suddenly, they ran into a thick, unforgiving wall of briars and thorns. The prickly, painful plants poked, grabbed, and tore at their skin and clothing. After several torturous minutes, they finally broke through the briar patch into open ground beyond. The younger of the two lads paused to catch his breath.

"Justus, I cannot keep going! I must rest!" begged eleven-year-old Jonas Avery. He knelt down, turned, and then collapsed, exhausted, against the base of a huge oak tree.

Justus Avery, three years older than Jonas, groaned in annoyed frustration. He urged his brother onward. "We cannot stop now, Brother! Old man Sledge and his blood-thirsty mongrels are right behind us!"

"We haven't heard any dogs for an hour or more," Jonas retorted. "And I haven't eaten anything since yesterday's supper. Please, Justus! I am so very tired. My legs are aching. Let me sit and catch my breath for just a while."

"Oh, all right! But, only for a very *short* while. We cannot risk lingering for very long. If we do, Sledge and his four-legged companions will surely catch us."

Justus sat down beside his little brother. He placed his linen carrying sack in his lap and inspected it to ensure that their most prized possession remained safe and intact. It was a small glass bottle that contained a very important piece of paper. It was their only remaining connection to their father. Thankfully, the bottle was unbroken, despite their treacherous and dangerous flight through the woods.

The night was cold, so Justus scooted nearer to his brother so that they might share the heat of their bodies. He immediately regretted the decision to stop and rest. His eyes were growing heavy. His body and mind longed for sleep.

"Do we have any more water?" begged Jonas, his voice little more than a whisper.

"No, brother. You already drank the last of it."

"There must be a creek around here somewhere," whined Jonas. He sat upright and peered thirstily into the impenetrable darkness that surrounded them.

"We cannot look for water in the dark, Jonas. It will be dawn in a few hours. Then we will find water and fill our canteens. Meanwhile, you must wait."

Jonas covered his eyes. He felt like crying. But this was certainly no time to cry. He and his brother had been through many more difficult circumstances during their five years in America. Surely, he could endure being hungry and thirsty until the sunrise. It was a small price to pay for his freedom.

JUSTUS AND JONAS AVERY, AGES FOURTEEN AND ELEVEN, had suffered terribly during their short lifetimes. Five years prior, in the spring of 1770, they set sail on the passenger ship, *Hope*, from the port of Liverpool, England. They traveled with their parents, Jeremiah and Anna Avery. The adventurous family departed their native land to go in search of a new life in the American Colonies. Their hearts had been filled with dreams of prosperity and plenty in the New World.

Sadly, not everyone on board their ship enjoyed as bright and promising a future as did the Avery boys. Many of the poorer people, including dozens of boys and girls, paid for their journey to the Colonies with the promise of future labor. Since they had no money to purchase passage to America, they had to agree to go across the sea as indentured servants.

Being an indentured servant was not the same as being a slave, but it was frighteningly close. Upon reaching America, impoverished travelers paid for their ship passage by committing to several years of physical labor. In addition to a "free" cross-Atlantic voyage, they received shelter and food during their time of service. After their years of servitude were complete, they would finally receive their freedom. Some of the luckier ones were indentured to weavers, shop workers, printers, or other professionals. However, most were indentured as servants on farms or plantations. Farm work was endless and back-breaking, and most field indentures suffered terrible conditions.

The process of selecting the indentured servants was also quite cruel. Upon the arrival of a ship filled with unpaid passengers, local businessmen and landowners would go on board and "shop" among the potential servants. Once they selected the laborers that they needed for their plantations or businesses, they paid the ship's captain the fee for their transport to America. Then, they took their newly purchased servants away to their new homes. Sometimes husbands and wives were separated from one another. In the worst of circumstances children were taken from their parents. It was an inhumane, heart-breaking way to begin a new life in the New World.

Jeremiah Avery had no intention of allowing his family to become indentured servants on some faraway Colonial plantation. He was trained as a cobbler, but he dreamed of owning his own farm. Though he did not mind making and repairing shoes, he desired something different. He wanted to get away from overcrowded cities and people. He longed for a piece of land that he could call his own ... a quiet place on the edge of the American wilderness.

Thankfully, Mr. Avery had always been a very wise and resourceful man. He worked hard and saved his money. Unlike most other travelers to America, he bought his family's ship passage with silver coin. He also paid in advance for the food they would eat while on board the ocean vessel. He even had a tidy sum of silver and gold stashed away to purchase land and farm equipment once they arrived in America. When they reached the port of Baltimore, Maryland, he would owe no one. He would pay cash for everything his family needed. The future of the Avery family seemed bright, indeed.

But the sea journey to the New World shattered all of their hopes and dreams. One week into the voyage Mrs. Avery became sick with a terrible fever. In a matter of days, the fever worked its way through almost every soul on board the ship. One-third of the passengers perished from the deadly disease. Sadly, there were no funerals or memorial services for those who died. The crewmen carried the bodies of the dead up onto the deck and then simply tossed them into the sea.

Justus and Jonas watched helplessly as their mother fought valiantly against the horrible sickness. She finally died after three days of fevered suffering. The sailors on the ship, anxious to stop the spread of the disease, immediately took her body away and cast it overboard into the roiling, stormy sea. The confused, heartbroken little boys did not even have the chance to say goodbye to their beloved mother.

The relentless sickness attacked many members of the boat's crewmen, as well. Captain Ichabod Rochelle, commander of the vessel, lost seventeen sailors during the course of the voyage. Some perished from the fever, but most died during a ferocious Atlantic storm. One huge wave in the frightening tempest washed almost a dozen sailors overboard. With the loss of so many seamen, the captain required fresh crewmen to work on his boat.

Jeremiah Avery, seeing the opportunity to earn some extra income, immediately signed on to serve as a member of the crew. In return for working throughout the remainder of the voyage, he contracted to receive a suitable wage as well as a private room for his sons. Each morning he left the boys safely in their cabin while he worked up on deck. In the evenings he returned and brought them their one meal for the day. For weeks this was their family routine. They made do as best they could and waited for the day when they would reach their new home.

Then, just before the ship reached America, tragedy struck the Avery family once more. Two days out of Baltimore, Jeremiah suffered a horrible fall from one of the ship's masts. The bones in both of his legs were shattered when he landed upon the deck. He also had a severe blow to his head. The poor man was unconscious when the ship arrived at the port.

Immediately, some of his fellow ship's crewmen volunteered to take Mr. Avery to a local doctor. Justus and Jonas watched, helpless and confused, as the sailors carried their injured father down the wobbly gangplank. Another fellow walked behind the stretcher bearers. He was carrying their father's travel trunk and his box of cobbling tools. As they were departing, one of the crewmen stopped, knelt in front of the boys, and placed a small glass bottle into nine-year-old Justus' hands.

The crusty old sailor explained, "Son, there is an important message for you inside this bottle. It tells the name of the doctor and the hospital where we are taking your papa. I asked the ship's surgeon to write it all down for you. As soon as the captain releases you from this boat, you must go there and find him." The sailor cut a distrusting glance at the ship's captain. He leaned closer and whispered, "But you must not trust the captain. He is an evil man. You must leave this ship and get away from him as quickly as you can. Do you understand?"

Justus did not really understand, but he nodded anyway. He assumed, in childlike faith, that the captain would eventually help him and his little brother to be reunited with their father. And why did the sailor call him an "evil man?" Captain Rochelle had always been kind to their family. It made no sense. So, he decided to place his trust in Captain Rochelle.

But little Justus had been terribly wrong. Instead of helping the grief-stricken boys, Captain Rochelle took advantage of them. He saw them as an opportunity to make some easy money. Since there were no parents or family members to challenge his intentions, the captain dishonestly changed the ship's log and listed the two boys as orphans. He stole their baggage and belongings. He pocketed the money that their father had paid for passage, along with the crewman's wages that he had earned. He then placed the helpless little boys for sale into indentured servitude.

Almost a week after the ship docked in Baltimore, a Virginia plantation owner named Benedict Dawson bought them. Since they were homeless, "orphan" children, their indentures would last until they reached the age of twenty-one ... an unthinkable twelve years for Justus and fifteen years for Jonas. The wicked Captain Rochelle had sold their entire childhood for a handful of silver coins.

Mr. Dawson ignored Justus and Jonas' pleas for help. He rejected their claims that they were not orphans, and that their father was alive and surely looking for them.

They tried to explain to the man what Captain Rochelle had done to them. Mr. Dawson threatened the boys with punishment if they did not cease their silly lies and accusations. The boys were so afraid that they stopped. They had no choice.

Needless to say, the Avery boys' lives changed dramatically. Life on the Dawson plantation was grim. It was made even more so by their evil and cruel foreman, Abram Sledge. Under his harsh and heartless supervision, Justus and Jonas suffered hunger, sickness, mistreatment, and frequent beatings with a leather strap. They were forced to work like grown men from sunup to sundown in the corn and tobacco fields. It was a horrible fate for two innocent little boys.

The only kindness they ever received was from Mr. Dawson's tender-hearted daughter, Drusilla. She was barely a year older than Justus. A few weeks after their arrival at the Dawson plantation, Drusilla formed a secret friendship with the boys. She helped care for them when they were sick. She gave them extra food, clothing, blankets, medicine, and shoes. Many evenings, after her father had gone to bed, she snuck away from her luxurious plantation house and made her way to the humble servant's quarters to play games with the boys. She was a true and good friend, constantly risking her father's wrath in order to give the Avery lads a little better life.

Even though they cared deeply for Drusilla, the boys still longed to be somewhere else. They wanted desperately to find their father and become a family again. Every night, as they lay together in their tiny bed in the darkness of their drafty, rickety shack, they recalled and shared stories from their early childhood. They tried to remember the faces of their mother and father. They did not want to forget them. They also prayed for their father each night, hoping beyond all hope that he was still alive and well. They prayed also that he was looking for them.

Occasionally, Justus would pull the ancient, dusty bottle from its hiding place beneath their bed. He and Jonas would remove the rolled-up piece of stained paper from the bottle and stare helplessly at its cryptic message. They talked and dreamed of escaping servitude and going out in search of their father. But how could they possibly find him? They could not read or write, so they did not even know the words of their message. And, since they were indentured servant laborers, they dared not ask anyone for help.

It was Drusilla who proved to be the answer to their dilemma. One night, after the three children had just enjoyed a candlelight game of dominoes, Jonas accidentally mentioned their secret message in the bottle. Justus was very upset that his little brother had revealed their secret and scolded him for doing so. It was a tense moment. After much coaxing, Drusilla finally convinced Justus to retrieve the bottle and show her the paper.

"I will read your secret message for you. I will not tell anyone," she promised.

Reluctantly, Justus retrieved the bottle, removed its cork, and took out the secret message. He unrolled the paper and handed it to Drusilla.

She smiled happily as she read the words. "It says, *'Almshouse Hospital – Dr. Thaddeus Hamilton.'*"

At long last, the boys knew the place where the sailors had taken their father. They memorized the words. They determined that somehow, someday, they would go there and find out what had happened to their father.

Drusilla, of course, insisted that she should help. She convinced the boys that they needed more than just determination and bravery to find their father. They needed to know how to read so that they could search for him in newspapers and other documents. So, she brought them an ancient, stained, torn copy of the *New England Primer* from her father's library. She used the book to teach the boys how to read. She also brought them her slate writing board and chalk so that they could learn to write. For three years, she secretly borrowed over a hundred other books from the library and loaned them to Justus and Jonas so that they might practice their reading skills. The boys learned quickly. Clearly, they each had a gift for language.

In the end, it was Drusilla who had helped them to finally make their decision to escape. The trio conspired together and decided that the Avery boys would flee the plantation after the break of winter, in late March of the year 1775. Throughout the cold, snowy months of January and February, Drusilla brought the boys food, salt, canteens, and extra stockings. She sewed coats for them from scraps of wool cloth. She even pilfered a map from her father's study and marked a path that would lead the boys eastward to the city of Baltimore. It would be a treacherous journey, and they would have to somehow cross the mighty Potomac River. But she was convinced that they could make it. They were, after all, resourceful and cunning young fellows.

The boys continued their normal, exhausting work activities under the watchful eye of the wicked Abram

Sledge each day. Then, at night, they organized their meager belongings and plotted their escape. Drusilla convinced them that the best night to go would be on March 28. That was the evening of the Frederick County Grand Ball. Her father and many of his workers and servants would be gone to the nearby town of Winchester to attend this dance. It was the biggest social event of the season. It was a perfect distraction and the ideal opportunity for them to make their getaway. Their only obstacle, if he did not attend the ball, would be the overseer, Abram Sledge, and his relentless pack of bloodhounds.

On the evening of March 27, the night before the ball, Drusilla stole away from the plantation house to enjoy one final visit with her friends. She brought them a half-loaf of fresh bread from the kitchen, two linen sacks to carry their belongings, and another very unexpected surprise. She gave Justus a tiny leather sack containing several English pennies and half-pennies, along with a few cut pieces of Spanish silver. It was an unimaginable treasure in coins. The boys had never seen so much money before. Justus protested and attempted to refuse the gift, but Drusilla insisted they take it.

Then, it was time for her to go. Their parting had been an emotional one. As they said their final goodbyes, Jonas cried like a baby, as did Drusilla. She gave them each one final hug and then kissed both of them on the cheek. Still crying, she lifted the crude wooden latch on the door and sprinted into the night. Both boys watched through a crack in the wall until she disappeared into the darkness of the nearby forest. It would be, they assumed, the last time that they would ever see their faithful friend, Drusilla Dawson.

Twenty-four hours later, the boys were gone from the plantation. They had escaped! They were on the run and heading east through the dense forests of northern Virginia. Unfortunately for them, Abram Sledge did not like dances and formal balls. Instead, he and his pack of hunting dogs were hot on the boys' trail.

❧

JUSTUS AWAKENED WITH A START. FOR A MOMENT HE could not remember where he was. But then the memories of their escape and flight through the Virginia woods quickly flooded his mind. He scolded himself angrily. He could not believe that he had dozed. He turned and looked at his brother. Jonas' head was resting against the moss-encrusted bark of the tree. The boy's mouth was wide open. He was snoring. A trickle of drool oozed down his chin.

"Jonas! Wake up! We must go!"

"Wha ... what?" Jonas stammered, wiping the sticky spit from his face.

"We fell asleep!" Justus exclaimed. "I cannot believe it! Both of us fell asleep!"

"Oh, no!" Jonas became frantic. "How long, do you reckon?"

"I don't know. But we have to go now! You can bet that Sledge and the hounds have not stopped to rest."

Suddenly, somewhere in the distant west, they heard the mournful howl of bloodhounds. It was their pursuers!

Jonas wailed, "It's Sledge! He is almost upon us! Oh, he will whip us, for sure!"

"Come on!" urged Justus. "We have to find a river or

creek. It's the only way we can throw the dogs off of our scent."

Both boys scrambled to their feet and then stumbled forward into the dark forest. Ahead of them, through the tangled limbs of the still-leafless trees, the pinkish-purple glow of dawn was just beginning to creep upward into the eastern sky.

2

TRICKERY

Daylight finally dispelled the darkness, enabling the runaway brothers to move more swiftly and safely through the woods. Though their legs were heavy with fatigue, they ran onward, hoping to put some distance between themselves and their relentless canine pursuers. But no matter how far they ran, Sledge and his dogs seemed to be steadily gaining ground. As the animals encountered the fresh scent of their quarry, their howls and barks increased in pitch and volume. At times, it sounded as if they were screaming, such was their excitement.

Justus suddenly stopped running. Jonas, not paying attention, slammed into his brother's back and then fell hard onto the ground.

"Why are you stopping?" wailed Jonas angrily. "Sledge is almost upon us!"

"Do you hear that?" Justus hissed.

Jonas strained to listen. Somewhere ahead, he heard

the sound of trickling water. He smiled. "It sounds like a creek."

Justus nodded. "Indeed. And a creek is exactly what we need. We can lose the dogs by walking in the water. They will not be able to smell us or follow our trail. Let's go!"

The boys ran onward. About fifty yards ahead, they encountered a tiny, bubbling creek. It flowed toward the north.

"Follow me," Justus commanded.

He leapt into the creek and then ran northward, in the direction of the downstream flow. Thankfully, the creek was very shallow, barely reaching over the tops of the boys' shoes. They ran through the frigid water for at least a half-mile before stopping to rest.

"I need a drink, and we need to fill our canteens," begged Jonas.

Justus nodded. Both boys bent over and cupped their hands in the crystal-clear water. They drank thirstily, downing several handfuls of the refreshing liquid. Once their thirst had been quenched, they each removed their two canteens and then began to fill them. The boys each carried an oak wooden canteen and a large, hollowed-out gourd. They filled their empty water jugs quickly. Afterwards, Jonas began to walk toward the nearest creekbank. He was eyeing a large boulder. The lad was tired, and it looked like a perfect place to sit and rest.

"Stop! Don't go near the edge!" warned Justus.

"Why?"

"Because, if you sit on that rock, the dogs will be able to find your scent. We must remain in the water."

"For how long?" whined Jonas. "This water is as cold as ice, and I can barely feel my feet."

Justus shrugged. "For as long as we can stand the cold, I suppose. Right now, we're wasting time. Let's move."

He turned and immediately trudged downstream. Jonas followed closely behind. As they worked their way down the creek, the dogs sounded more and more distant. It seemed that their plan to trick the animals was working. However, they soon encountered another difficulty. As the elevation descended, the water became deeper. After almost a mile, it was well above their knees.

"This water is almost betwixt my legs," groaned Jonas. "Isn't it time that we get out of this creek?"

"Yes," replied his brother. "I suppose we must. Let's find a clear spot on the eastern bank and then we will head for dry ground."

The boys quickly found a break in the vegetation along the water's edge and immediately exited the freezing cold water. Soon, they were moving toward the east once again. The forest floor was wide open and covered with hard-packed leaves. It made for easy travel. They marched onward for two hours, pausing only three times to catch their breath and take a drink of water. It was almost noon when they came upon a small, rock-covered hill. On the southern side of the hill, a tiny spring bubbled fresh water into a clear pool. It was the perfect spot to rest and, once again, top off their canteens. Thankfully, they could no longer hear the dogs.

Jonas leaned, exhausted, against the soft, moss-covered hillside. Filling his canteens would have to wait. He needed a rest. Justus felt the same. He reclined on the ground beside his brother. They lay still for several minutes before either of them spoke.

Jonas finally asked, "How far do you think we are from the Potomac River?"

"I have no idea. But we will find it sooner or later if we keep moving to the north and east."

"I'm hungry," Jonas declared, changing the subject altogether.

"I, as well, but there is no food to be had out here in the woods. If it were summer, we might find some berries. If it were fall, there would be nuts all over the ground. But, with the recent passing of winter, nothing edible remains. The animals have surely cleaned everything out." He paused. "Do not worry, Brother. We will get something to eat sooner or later. Thanks to Drusilla, if we can find us a village or tavern, we have plenty of money to purchase a hot meal."

"But we don't know how long that will be," Jonas whined.

"No, we don't. But, rest assured, we will not be wandering about in the wilderness forever."

Suddenly, the boys heard an odd scratching sound. Then came a low rumble. It almost sounded like a growl. The sound emanated from the north, somewhere beyond the far side of the hill where they lay. Then came another strange noise. It sounded like a baby crying, but much lower in pitch and volume.

Jonas sat up and cocked his head to one side. "What the devil was that?"

His older brother's eyes were wide with fear. "It sounded like a critter of some sort."

"What manner of critter?" demanded Jonas.

"I think it was a bear."

"A bear?" Jonas exclaimed. "Surely, you are mistaken!"

The younger lad scrambled to his feet and ran to the top of the hill. A couple hundred yards to the northwest he saw something big and black loping through the woods. Two smaller creatures followed closely behind. Almost immediately, Justus joined him on the hilltop.

The older lad nodded. "Yep. It is just as I suspected ... it is a mama black bear and her cubs. It looks like they are moving away from us, thank goodness. They probably haven't been awake for very long."

"What do you mean?"

"Bears sleep all winter. In the springtime, they wake up and come out of their dens."

"How in the world do you know that?" asked Jonas, somewhat confused. "We have never even seen a bear before today."

Justus shrugged. "It was in one of the books that Drusilla brought us." He scanned the area around them. Soon, he pointed toward a large hole in the side of a nearby gully. "That is probably their den right over there. Bears sleep underground, you know."

Jonas shook his head in disbelief. "I must not have read that book."

Suddenly and quite unexpectedly, far to the southwest, they heard the faint, distant yelp of a dog. As the seconds passed, the barking grew closer.

"It's Sledge!" Jonas hissed angrily. "He must have followed the creekbank downstream until the hounds picked up our scent. What are we going to do now?"

Justus did not answer. He was staring thoughtfully at the entrance to the bear's den.

Jonas snapped his fingers in front of his brother's face.

"What's wrong with you, Justus? Are you in some sort of trance? We must flee! The dogs will soon be upon us!"

Justus turned and faced his brother. He smiled. "I think I have a plan."

THE BOYS WERE STANDING IN THE BOTTOM OF THE gully. The ground all around them was covered with bear scat. Clearly, it was the place where the mama bear had deposited her droppings throughout the long winter.

"You want to do *what?*" Jonas exclaimed in disbelief.

Justus pointed at a particularly large pile of fresh, steaming bear dung. "We are going to rub the scat all over our bodies and then crawl into that hole and hide in the bear's den. The smell of the dung combined with the musky smell of bear will cover our scent. It should really confuse the dogs."

Jonas shook his head emphatically. He squealed, "There is no way I am going to do that! That there is a nasty pile of bear manure!" He pointed at the den. "And there is no way I'm climbing into that dark hole in the ground! There's no telling what might be hiding in there!"

"Bear scat is not like manure from a cow or horse." Justus knelt beside the pile and scooped up a handful of the reddish-black dung. He lifted it to his nose and sniffed. "This bear ate wild berries and hickory nuts. That's what it smells like. It is not all that unpleasant an odor."

Jonas stared incredulously at his brother. "I do believe that you have lost your mind."

The barking of the dogs was getting louder. The pack of hounds was dangerously close.

Justus stood and confronted Jonas. "Do you have any better ideas? Sledge will be here soon. We are both exhausted. We can't outrun them. I honestly believe this is our only hope of escape. We must use our wits. We must use trickery."

Jonas inhaled a deep, frustrated breath. He cut his eyes at his brother. "This is going to ruin our clothes; I hope you know."

Justus grinned. "They are already ripped to shreds, anyway. Once we get across the river, we will find us some new clothes."

Again, Jonas shook his head in disgust. "All right, then. Let's get to it."

❦

THE BOYS HUDDLED TOGETHER SILENTLY, DEEP INSIDE the bear's den. It was not as they had expected. A narrow, horizontal tube extended about eight feet into the hillside and then opened up into a slightly larger "room." It was surprisingly comfortable and quite warm. Outside, they could hear the dogs getting closer. It sounded as if the rowdy hounds were almost upon them.

"Did you cover our tracks well enough?" Jonas asked, worried. "All this manure will be of no use at all if they see shoe prints leading into the bear hole."

Justus gave his brother a reassuring pat on the leg. "Do not worry. I covered our tracks very well. I used pine boughs to scatter the dirt and leaves all the way up to the entrance of the den. They will never know that we are in here."

There was a brief moment of silence.

"This place doesn't smell right," Jonas complained in a hoarse whisper.

Justus grinned and gave his brother a friendly nudge. "You are the one who doesn't smell right."

The howling, screeching dogs arrived just outside the entrance to the den. Soon came the sound of human voices.

"Shush!" Justus hissed quietly. "Not another word."

The boys lay absolutely still and silent. They prayed that the men and their dogs would simply go away. But, instead, they lingered in the area for several minutes. The barking decreased, however, as the dogs sniffed the ground and searched for the scent of the runaway boys.

Suddenly, a high-pitched, whiny, irritating voice spoke from somewhere very near to the den's entrance. It was the unmistakable voice of John Bailey, Abram Sledge's assistant. Actually, the pesky little man was little more than the overseer's lackey. He took care of the hunting dogs and did other odd jobs for Sledge. Mostly, however, he was the plantation tattletale. He was always informing on the servants and slaves and getting them into trouble with the overseer. He was universally despised by every worker on the Dawson farm.

Bailey chirped, "Something's wrong with your dogs, Mr. Sledge."

"They've lost the scent! That is what's wrong with these worthless hounds!" Sledge responded in frustration.

"Reckon why, Mr. Sledge?"

"I don't know!" Sledge snapped angrily. "They had a good, strong scent right up until we reached this gully. Now, they're all confused. Just look at them! They are wandering about in circles and sniffing the wind."

There was a pause in the conversation. Finally, John Bailey spoke again. "There is bear manure all over the place, Mr. Sledge. Reckon it's all the bear scent down in this gully that has stymied the hounds?"

"That's actually some good thinking, John," Sledge responded, sounding surprised. "Look! You can see where the ground in front of that den has been disturbed. I'll bet there is a skinny old bear nearby that is fresh awake from the winter. The critter has likely been roaming all over this ground, probably with a cub or two trailing close behind. My dogs will never be able to smell those boys here amongst all these strange odors." He groaned. "We must get the dogs back on their trail! We simply have to find them!"

"What will happen if we don't bring the boys back? Reckon what Mr. Dawson might do? Will he get rid of us for failing?" John Bailey's voice sounded shaky and fearful. "Mr. Sledge, I can't get fired. I need this job."

"Do not worry. Neither of us will lose our jobs," Sledge reassured him. "Besides, I never planned on bringing these two boys back to the plantation, anyway."

"What do you mean?" asked John. He sounded confused. "Why would you not bring them back?"

"Can you keep a secret, John?"

"Yes, sir." He paused and then asked, "What kind of secret?"

Mr. Sledge's voice dropped slightly in pitch and volume, as if he were afraid that someone besides John Bailey might hear him. He declared, "John, not long ago I heard Mr. Dawson say that the father of these two boys was sitting on a sack full of Spanish silver and gold. The man possesses a great treasure!"

John Bailey whistled, impressed. "But how would Mr. Dawson know something like that? And besides, I thought these boys were orphans straight off of the boat."

"No, that was all a lie. Their papa was hurt on the ship and taken to a hospital when they docked. After that, Captain Rochelle sold the boys as indentures to Mr. Dawson. He and that crooked old boat captain are friends. Rochelle shared with Mr. Dawson that this Avery fellow, the father of these lads, told him all about his treasure and how he was going to buy himself land in America." He chuckled. "From the very beginning the captain had plans to take that money."

"But surely, he has already found the treasure and taken it for himself," reasoned John.

"No, he has not," declared Sledge happily. "I saw a letter on Mr. Dawson's desk about a month ago. It was from Captain Rochelle. They have kept in contact with one another over the years. He informed Mr. Dawson that he had not been able to track this Avery fellow down. By the time he got to the hospital where the sailors left him, the man was already gone and there was nothing to show where he went. Captain Rochelle was hoping that the boys might know something. That's why he wrote to Mr. Dawson to start with. It seems that our master and that crooked old sailor are in cahoots with one another. They both want to get their hands on Avery's silver and gold."

"So, then, the treasure is still out there somewhere?" John Bailey whined excitedly. "Just a waiting to be found?"

"It certainly is," Sledge answered. "And the father of these two runaway boys still has it. So, you and I are going to catch them, find their pappy, and then use the lads to get at that silver and gold!"

"Do you think your plan will actually work?"

"I know it will work," Sledge responded. "All we need to do is to put a knife to the throat of one of his boys and old Mr. Avery will start singing like a bird. Surely, he cares more about his own sons than any treasure. But to make my plan work we have to find those lads. First, we must get these dogs back on their scent."

"And we need to get far away from this nest of bears. But which way should we go?"

There was a pause as the men looked around and pondered their situation.

"I suspect the boys will head north from here," surmised Mr. Sledge. "We will go that way. Sooner or later, the dogs will find their trail."

John Bailey giggled excitedly. "Let's go catch those little scoundrels and then find us that treasure!"

Justus and Jonas listened silently as the men gathered their hounds. They did not dare speak as long as they could hear the dogs barking and howling. Finally, after almost a half-hour, the noises ceased. Their pursuers were gone.

Jonas elbowed his big brother. "Did you hear what old man Sledge said?"

"I heard."

"Do you think it is true?"

"I don't know," Justus responded quietly. "I never heard Father speak of such things. But, in the end, none of that talk of gold or treasure really matters. The only thing that matters to us is finding our papa. Agreed?"

"Agreed," answered Jonas. "So, where do we go now?"

"We head due east, toward the Potomac. We will be far

away from Sledge and his dogs before the sun sets. Tomorrow, hopefully, we can cross the river into Maryland."

"And wash all of this bear scat off of us," added Jonas.

Justus grinned. He began crawling out of the den. "Indeed. Come on. Let's go. We need to reach Baltimore as quickly as possible. We need to find the *Almshouse Hospital*. They should have a clue that will lead us to Papa."

3
THE CABIN

It was early afternoon. The boys walked toward the east. And since they had escaped Sledge and his dogs, they moved at a much slower and more relaxed pace. Still, for safety's sake, they paused often to listen for the barking of bloodhounds. Thankfully, they heard none.

About two hours after departing their hideout in the underground bear's den, they came upon a large creek. The meandering, snake-like waterway held deep water in numerous crystal-clear pools. The boys paused and stared longingly at the clean, inviting water.

Jonas nudged his older brother. "You thinking what I'm thinking?"

Justus grinned. "Bath time?"

"Yes, sir!" exclaimed Jonas. "I am ready to be rid of this bear scat. No matter what you say, I still think it smells rank." The lad was already stripping off his manure-encrusted clothing.

"Let's place our clothes in the water to soak for a bit whilst we wash ourselves."

Jonas nodded. "Good idea."

Both boys stripped off all of their filthy garments and carried them a few yards downstream. They placed them in a shallow pool and weighed them down with large rocks. Then, they trudged back upstream to a particularly large pool of water. It was actually deep enough for swimming. Both boys immediately dived in. However, they did not remain submerged for long. The water was so frigid that it took their breath away.

"This is too cold for me!" exclaimed Jonas as soon as his head popped above the water.

"You will get used to it in a minute." Justus pointed toward a bright, sunny spot about twenty yards to the south. "After we wash, we can rest over there in the sun and get warm."

The lads immediately began to scrub their filthy bodies. Besides being covered with bear manure, they also stunk from several days of dirt, filth, and sweat. They each found small, flat pieces of gritty sandstone along the creek-bank and used the stones to scrub their skin. The method was crude but effective. Despite having no soap, they soon had their bodies washed smooth and clean.

Their hair, however, was another challenge altogether. It took much longer to clean their unkempt manes. Both Justus and Jonas had long hair, as was typical for boys in the 1700's. Each of them wore their hair pulled back into a pony-tail queue. After two days on the run through dense woods, their hair had come untied and become matted and tangled. The only tool that they possessed for hair care was one half of a broken ox horn comb that Jonas carried in his linen sack.

They soaked and scrubbed their hair for several

minutes. After the soaking, each boy took turns picking the tangles from the other's hair with the ancient comb. It was a long and sometimes painful process. But, eventually, each brother had the other's hair detangled and tied once again into a proper, orderly queue.

The boys did not linger for long in their bathing pool. They swam downstream and quickly retrieved their clothes. The lengthy soaking in the moving water had loosened and washed away much of the bear scat. However, to get their clothing completely clean would still require some scrubbing. They dragged all of their garments to the creekbank, located two large, flat rocks, and then went to work on their laundry. They pounded each garment with slabs of sandstone and methodically scrubbed away the filth. It took several washings and rinses before they could officially declare their laundry clean enough to wear.

"I'm freezing," Justus declared through chattering teeth. "Let us go and lie down in that sunny spot."

The boys dragged their coats, weskits, shirts, breeches, and stockings from the creek. They gave each garment a thorough squeeze to wring out the excess water and then darted toward the warmth of the sun. They hung their clothes on limbs and branches, making sure that each garment was fully exposed to the sunshine. Then, they reclined lazily on the soft, leaf-covered ground, allowing the sun to bathe their bodies with its comforting warmth. It was not long before both boys were fast asleep.

JONAS AWAKENED WITH A SHIVER. HE SAT UP, STRETCHED lazily, and then scanned the forest around him. Everything appeared peaceful and quiet. He glanced at the sky. He could tell by the shadows in the treetops that the sun would be going down soon. They had less than two hours of daylight remaining. He reached to his left and gave his brother a quick poke in the arm.

"Nap time is over, Justus. We need to find shelter before it gets dark."

The elder of the Avery boys sat up slowly, stretched, and yawned. He turned to his little brother and smiled. "That was a good sleep. I needed it."

"Indeed," responded Jonas. "But I fear that we have slept too long. Our daylight is almost gone, and we haven't even reached the Potomac yet."

"It will be all right," his brother reassured him. He stood and gathered his dry clothes. "Let's get dressed and then find a place to spend the night. We can cross the river in the morning."

The boys dressed quickly and then headed east, following the creek as it wound its way through the woods. They assumed that the tiny waterway would lead them to the Potomac River. Sure enough, about a half-hour later they emerged from the forest along the banks of the famous river. The opposite bank on the Maryland side was at least a hundred yards distant.

Jonas whistled quietly. "Brother, that is one wide river. How will we ever get across?"

"We will find a way," Justus proclaimed confidently. "But that is a task for tomorrow. Right now, we need to find some manner of shelter. It's getting colder."

"Some supper would be nice," added Jonas.

Justus shook his head grimly. "Don't get your hopes up."

Jonas glanced left and right. "Which way should we go?"

"Let's head south."

The boys turned to their right and walked along a tiny path that followed the riverbank. After several minutes of walking, Jonas asked, "Does this trail look animal or human to you?"

"Definitely human. I saw an iron ring and some sawed lumber beside the trail a little while ago."

"Then, do you think there is a homestead nearby?" Jonas inquired hopefully.

Justus shrugged. "It would not surprise me."

They marched onward. Darkness was descending rapidly, along with the temperature. The boys were shivering from the cold. They were becoming desperate to find shelter. They soon spotted a side trail.

"That trail is turning away from the river," whispered Justus. "Let's see where it goes."

The boys walked stealthily, straining to see or hear anything that might seem out of place. The new trail turned sharply to their right as it entered the tree line. They proceeded carefully. After walking a short distance, Justus suddenly dropped to one knee. Jonas did the same.

"What is it? What did you see?" hissed Jonas. Fear filled his voice.

"There is a small cabin and outbuildings in the clearing up ahead," answered Justus.

"Did you see any smoke coming from the chimney?"

Justus shook his head.

"Did you see any people?"

"No. Still, we must be careful." Justus paused as he scanned the woods and considered their situation. "I am going to go and scout the area. You stay here and wait for my signal."

Jonas nodded obediently. Without another word, Justus darted silently down the trail that led to the cabin. He was gone for several minutes. Jonas was just beginning to worry when Justus suddenly appeared out of the darkness. He was walking upright and smiling. He waved to his brother. Jonas stood to greet him.

"Well ... what did you find? Is anyone in the cabin?"

Justus shook his head. "No. It is long abandoned."

"Did you go inside?"

"I did, indeed. It is warm and dry. The fireplace looks good, too. I think it will draw just fine. There is even an old stack of firewood beside the door." He paused, grinning. "And I found about two dozen ears of dried corn in a rickety corn crib."

Jonas' eyes widened. He exclaimed happily, "Supper!"

"I also discovered a small iron pot in the shed. It needs a little cleaning to get the rust out, but it should serve us well. All we need is a fire. Then we shall enjoy some boiled corn."

"I'm starving! Let's go!" urged Jonas. He pushed past his brother and darted in the direction of the old cabin.

THEIR CORN SUPPER HAD BEEN MORE OF A CHALLENGE than they had expected. Justus got the fire started easily enough, but the ancient ears of corn in the nearby corn crib were in pretty bad shape. Some of them were moldy.

Others had been partially eaten by rats and mice. The boys had to pick carefully through all of the ears to separate the good pieces of grain. Once they had a sizable pile of edible kernels, they next had to crack the dried grain for cooking. Using a small rock for pounding, they smashed the corn on a large slab of rock that they discovered near the cabin door. Once all of the kernels were cracked, they tossed them into the pot. The boys covered the grain with clean water, poured in a generous dose of salt from Jonas' salt horn, and then hung the pot over the fire to boil.

Since there were no eating utensils inside the old cabin, the boys decided to carve a set of spoons. They needed something to do besides sitting and staring at the boiling pot. They searched the meager woodpile until each of them found a suitable piece of wood. Then, they took out their pocketknives and went to work. They whittled the wood into shapes that vaguely resembled spoons and then set about the more intricate carving of the round-shaped bowl. They turned the activity into a fun competition, each boy attempting to produce a "perfect" spoon.

One hour later, they were ready to enjoy their hot, satisfying supper with their brand-new, freshly carved oak wood spoons. Of course, neither utensil was perfect. The spoons were rough and splintery and would certainly never pass as spoons in the "civilized world," but they worked just fine in their abandoned Virginia cabin. The boys proudly and happily used their hand-carved creations to shovel the salty corn mush into their hungry mouths. They quickly emptied the pot of every morsel of the satisfying, hot food.

After supper they brought in armloads of dry pine needles to construct a pallet on the cabin's dirt floor. They made their bed directly in front of the fireplace. For pillows they emptied their belongings from their linen sacks and then stuffed the sacks full of crushed leaves and pine needles. Since there were no blankets of tarps to be found, they would simply cover themselves with their overcoats.

Just before lying down, they filled the fireplace with several large logs so that the fire would burn throughout the entire night. Finally, the exhausted boys kicked off their shoes and then reclined upon their luxuriously soft makeshift bed. They sighed and rubbed their satisfied bellies as their tired bodies absorbed the warmth from the roaring, toasty fire. They had never felt so happy, content, and free. Despite their long afternoon nap, their eyes were heavy from exhaustion. Both lads were looking forward to a long, warm, restful night of good sleep. After two treacherous days on the run in the Virginia woods they had earned it.

As usual, Jonas began to fall asleep almost immediately, but Justus remained restless. His mind was always working. He was busy formulating plans. As the older brother of the two he bore a great amount of responsibility. He was determined to do anything he had to in order to find their father and get his little brother to safety.

"Jonas, are you asleep?"

"Yes!" his little brother groaned, sounding frustrated.

"I've been thinking ..."

"You're always thinking. Go to sleep. You can think tomorrow."

"Listen to me, Jonas. This is important."

The younger lad sighed impatiently. He flopped over

onto his side and faced his brother. "What is so all-fired important that you must talk about it tonight?"

"I have been thinking about what old man Sledge said ... about Papa and his treasure."

Jonas' eyes widened. Immediately, his head popped up from his pillow and he sat upright. "You have my attention."

"I believe now that we *must* go after the treasure," Justus declared.

"But you said before that we should not worry about such things. All we want to do is find Papa."

Justus nodded. "True. But, as I have considered everything, I have come to realize that to do one is to do the other. They are one in the same."

"Huh?" Jonas inquired. He was very confused.

Justus signed impatiently. "Don't you see? Wherever Papa is, that is where we will find his silver and gold. So, if hunting for this treasure gets us one step closer to finding him, it will be worth the effort. The treasure might even give us a clue as to where we might find him."

Jonas turned and stared into the glowing yellow-orange coals in the fireplace. A tiny tear formed in his eye. "Papa is the only treasure that I need. I miss him so very much."

"Not long ago you said that you could barely even remember him," Justus teased.

Jonas turned his eyes back to his brother. "That does not make me miss him any less. I remember the feeling of him holding me." He closed his eyes. "I even remember his smell."

"He always smelled like pipe tobacco," Justus said, smiling fondly.

Jonas grinned. "And Mama always smelled like lavender and mint."

Both boys became quiet and sad as they thought of their sweet mother. No matter how hard they tried, they could never forget the image of the sailors on board the ship carrying her body away.

"And there is one other reason that we need to find Papa's silver and gold," Justus announced.

"Why is that?"

Justus narrowed his eyes determinedly. "To keep Sledge and his little tattletale from getting their hands on it."

Jonas nodded slowly and thoughtfully. "That's for sure! We cannot allow them to find it. That would be a horrible injustice."

"It is going to be very difficult. Sledge will, no doubt, continue to pursue us. He will chase us all the way to Baltimore and beyond. You heard him. He wants to *use* us to get the treasure."

"Well, then, we shall just have to stay one step ahead of him," Jonas whispered confidently. "But running from Sledge and looking for Papa and his treasure will require much energy and effort." He turned his back toward his brother and then plopped back down onto his mattress of pine needles. "So, you must quit all this thinking and scheming and go to sleep."

The Next Morning

THE SUN WAS BARELY UP. THE BOYS STOOD ON THE

riverbank and stared dejectedly at the rain-swollen Potomac.

"Any ideas, Mr. Thinker?" Jonas whined sarcastically.

Justus surveyed their situation. "We must make a raft. We need about seven or eight short logs. We can lash them together with vines. Then, all we have to do is push off from the bank and then float across."

Jonas grunted skeptically. "We can't just float across. We need paddles of some kind. The current of this raging river could wash us all the way out to the Atlantic Ocean!"

"Well, do you have a better plan?" Justus challenged.

"No."

"All right, then. Let's get to work. We need to hunt for driftwood logs and wood for paddles. You go to the right and check downstream, and I will go left and check upstream. Give a shout if you see anything useful."

Jonas nodded. The boys parted quickly and went in search of lumber and supplies for constructing their raft. They had been searching for about a half hour when Justus suddenly heard a frantic, excited shout. It was his brother! He instantly took off running in the direction of Jonas' voice, fearful that something horrible had happened. He sprinted past a small cluster of trees and soon spotted him. Immediately, he realized why Jonas had been shouting so wildly. He was sitting inside a small rowboat. The tiny boat was tied to a large tree on the riverbank. The young lad was grinning from ear-to-ear and holding two small oars high in the air.

"I think I have a better plan," Jonas declared victoriously.

THE BOYS BEACHED THE "BORROWED" CRAFT ON A SMALL sandbar on the eastern riverbank. They quickly pulled the boat from the water and then concealed it in some tall grass. They hid in the grass and scanned the area for any sign of people or activity. They saw no one. Both boys breathed a sigh of relief.

"Are we in Maryland?" asked Jonas, still staring at the opposite riverbank.

His brother nodded. "We are, indeed."

"So ... what now?" asked Jonas.

Justus rubbed his belly. "My corn porridge is long gone. First, we go and find us a hot breakfast. Then we will head for Baltimore."

Jonas grinned happily. "What are we waiting for? Let's go!"

4
CHARITY

The boys traveled eastward through fields and woods. Unfortunately for them, there was no breakfast to be found. Around mid-morning they intersected a rutted, muddy highway. Assuming that Baltimore was north and east of them, they followed the road northward.

"Do you reckon we will find a town soon?" asked Jonas. "I'm getting mighty hungry."

"I should think so." Justus pointed at the wagon ruts in the dirt. "This is a much-traveled highway. It must lead someplace."

Minutes later, after rounding a bend in the road, they discovered a sign that read, "*Upper Marlborough – One Mile*."

Jonas happily punched his brother in the shoulder and then exclaimed, "Finally! I can taste my dinner already!"

IT WAS HALF-PAST NOON. JUSTUS AND JONAS OCCUPIED A small table in a dark corner inside the noisy, crowded *Sleeping Bear Tavern*. There were two other similar taverns located on the same street in Upper Marlborough, but Jonas had insisted that they dine at the *Sleeping Bear*. He loved the wooden sign that hung over the tavern's door. It was a carved image of a large black bear curled into a ball and fast asleep. It reminded him, of course, of their recent adventure in their bear's den hideaway.

The tavern girl who served them was an attractive, blonde-haired, green-eyed lass. She spoke with a slightly Scottish accent and appeared to be about the same age as Justus. She brought each of them a large pewter plate loaded with roasted goose and potatoes, corn porridge, and green peas. She also placed a loaf of warm bread on a wooden platter in the center of the table, along with a dish of creamy butter. Their beverages consisted of fresh milk. The milk was warm, delicious, and straight from the cow. The boys attacked their meals ravenously.

"So, what now? Where do we go?" asked Jonas, his cheeks swelled full of bread and meat.

Justus glanced around the room to make sure no one was within earshot. He whispered, "We must get to Baltimore as quickly as possible. It cannot be far."

"Why are you whispering?"

Justus gave his brother a stern look. "Because you never know who might be listening to our conversation. We need to keep our business to ourselves."

Jonas nodded and then continued to wolf down his food. Clearly, he was more interested in filling his belly than he was in conversing. The boys finished the remainder of their meal without any further talk. They ate every morsel on their plates and then sopped the pewter clean with chunks of bread. Once finished, they had little desire to tarry at the tavern. Both boys were anxious to get on the road to Baltimore.

"Let's get going right away," Justus urged. "But first we need to get directions to Baltimore and then cover as many miles as we can before dark."

"Should we not order some extra food to take with us for our supper tonight?" asked Jonas.

Justus' eyes lit up. "That is a fine idea, Brother! We must ask that young maid to bring us some more vittles for the road."

He turned around and soon made eye contact with the tavern girl. He waved to her in a polite gesture, inviting her to report to their table. The young lady seemed preoccupied by a piece of paper that she was holding in her hand. After a few seconds she hastily folded the paper and then stuffed it inside her apron pocket. Glancing left and right, she walked swiftly toward the boys.

As she neared their table, Justus announced, "Miss, might you be so kind as to prepare us some more ..."

The girl interrupted him abruptly, "You lads need to come with me right now." She spoke in a low, secretive voice.

Jonas shot his brother an alarmed, confused glance.

"Pardon me, Miss. We merely need to purchase some supper to take on the road with us. We are travelers, and anxious to be on our way."

Shaking her head, the girl hissed, "You must come with me now! Follow me through the kitchen. Keep your heads low. You do not wish to be recognized."

She turned and immediately walked toward the door

that led into the kitchen. Justus and Jonas grabbed their coats and their cocked hats and followed closely behind. The girl marched quickly though the kitchen and then out the back door of the tavern. She guided the brothers through a maze of sheds and outbuildings. They passed through a small gate behind the tavern's smokehouse that led to a narrow alleyway beyond. Once the gate was closed and latched, she stopped and spun around to face the boys. She whipped a crumpled piece of paper from her apron and waved it threateningly in front of Justus' face.

"I want you to explain this! Who are you, and why is there a reward for your capture?"

Justus was thoroughly perplexed. He slowly received the paper from her hand and then examined it. All of the color drained from his face. He shook his head in disbelief.

"What is it, Justus?" demanded his little brother.

"It is a handbill with our likenesses on it. It appears we have a bounty on our heads."

"Ten pounds sterling!" chirped the tavern maid, her head bobbing up and down excitedly. "That is more money than I have earned in the past year!"

"Ten pounds?" Jonas queried in disbelief. He snatched the paper from his brother's hand. The paper read, "*REWARD. Ten Pounds Sterling for the Capture of Two Runaway Indentures. To Be Paid by Benedict Dawson, Esquire – Frederick County, Virginia.*" The reward poster included their names, descriptions, and a very crude hand-drawn image of two boys.

"That does not look like us at all!" Jonas exclaimed, giggling. "It looks like a little child drew it."

"'Tis close enough," retorted the girl. "I recognized you immediately. Seeing two boys your age wandering about all alone is strange enough, especially when they are two filthy ragamuffins such as yourselves. Sooner or later, someone else beside me will figure out who you are."

"Where did you get this?" Jonas inquired.

"These handbills are hanging all over town. A skinny little fellow with a whiny, high-pitched voice brought this one to the tavern barely an hour before you arrived."

Jonas and Justus glanced knowingly at one another.

"John Bailey," groaned Jonas.

"Who is John Bailey?" asked the girl, obviously confused.

Justus inhaled deeply and shook his head in disgust. "He is the assistant overseer on our old plantation." He frowned as he looked at Jonas. "Old man Sledge must be here as well. Their dogs must have picked up our trail at the river."

"Or maybe they are just visiting all the towns up and down the river and passing out these handbills," Jonas responded optimistically.

The girl interrupted their conversation. "Someone had better tell me what is going on, and I mean right now!" she demanded. "And explain to me why I should not turn you in, myself, and claim this handsome reward."

Justus turned to the girl, removed his hat, and then bowed slightly. "Please pardon my horrible manners. I am Justus Avery, and this is my brother, Jonas. Might I ask your name?"

"Charity MacLellan."

Justus nodded politely. "Miss MacLellan, we are truly honored to meet you. Jonas and I are, indeed, runaways. But we are the victims of a grave injustice. Many years ago, we were unlawfully removed from our father and then sold into servitude. Just this past week, we fled our plantation to go in search of him. We hope to be reunited with him soon."

Charity's countenance darkened. She appeared sad. She lowered her chin to her chest and nodded her understanding. "I, too, am indentured. My father died when I was very young. My mother could not afford to feed us all, so she released my brother and myself into servitude. I have worked for the tavern owner since I was eight years old."

"What about your brother? Where is he?" asked Jonas.

She shook her head. "I have no notion of where Andrew might be. I have not seen him since the day we were separated at the county courthouse." She paused, appearing to be on the edge of tears. "I once heard a rumor that he had been taken to sea, but I do not know if it is true. I can only pray that I might see him again someday." She paused. "Well, Mama died a few years back. I think she died of a broken heart from having sent us away."

Justus nodded knowingly. "So, then, you understand our situation all too well."

Charity smiled warmly. "I do, indeed."

"Will you help us, then?" pleaded Jonas.

She eyed the older of the brothers. Justus' clothing was tattered and filthy and his long, unbrushed hair was a mess. She smiled mischievously.

"You two almost appear beyond help. Your clothes are nasty. And Good Heavens! Your hair! It looks like two coons got tangled up in a fight and then one of them died on top of your head." She covered her mouth with her hand and giggled. "Perhaps you should just shave it all off and start over."

Justus' face flushed red with embarrassment. He was a handsome lad, tall for his age and lean. His soft freckles matched perfectly with his reddish-brown hair. He was greatly disappointed that this beautiful young girl saw him as filthy and unkempt.

"Please pardon our appearance, Miss MacLellan," Justus pleaded sheepishly. "We have been on the run through wilderness lands for many days."

"I was only teasing you, Justus. Of course, I will help you. And please ... call me Charity. But first we must hide you away until nightfall. No doubt there will be many men anxious to find you and claim that reward. I heard some fellows talking about it inside the tavern." She pointed to her right. "Walk along this alley to the next block. Turn left and then follow the dirt road out of the town. About a half-mile to the north, you will cross a small bridge over a lovely little creek. Turn right just past the creek and follow the walking path into the woods. You will find an abandoned house beside the creek about a quarter-mile down the path. Wait there for me. I will come after dark with food and supplies for you."

"I do not know how we can ever repay you," Jonas declared, his eyes filling with joyful tears.

"There is nothing to repay. 'Tis the Christian thing to do. However, I must have payment for your meal. My master is not kind if I come up short on my receipts. Last week I lost two pence." She paused sorrowfully. "He whipped me good."

Justus fished the small leather coin pouch from his weskit pocket. He took out a small silver coin and handed it to Charity. "Will that cover our meal plus extra food for tonight and for the journey tomorrow?"

She smiled and nodded. "With plenty to spare."

"Thank you, Charity," Jonas said, extending his hand in friendship.

Charity shook his plump, dirty hand. "You are most welcome, Jonas." She glanced left and right. "Now, go. Get to the hideout. I will come as soon as I am able." Without another word, she darted through the gate and then closed it behind her.

"Let's get out of here!" Justus hissed. He turned and then sprinted down the alleyway. Jonas ran behind him.

❧

THE OLD HOUSE WAS EXACTLY WHERE CHARITY HAD told them. It was a small brick home concealed in a deep thicket of overgrown cedars. It did not appear that anyone had lived there for many years. All of the windows were boarded shut from the inside. There was an enormous iron lock on the front door. Justus and Jonas concealed themselves in the underbrush for several minutes and kept watch over the house as they considered their next move.

"Do you see anything suspicious?" whispered Jonas.

Justus shook his head. "I think it is abandoned."

Jonas eyed the house with suspicion. "I wonder why no one lives here. It looks like it was once a lovely little house."

Justus shrugged. "Who knows? But it will definitely be a comfortable place for us to spend the night."

"If we can find a way in," added his little brother skeptically.

Justus grinned and then stood upright. "Rest assured, I will get us in. Let's check around back."

A few minutes later, the boys discovered a way into the house. There was a loose board over a small window near the rear door. They pushed the board out of the way and then squeezed through the opening. Justus went first. Seconds later, Jonas tumbled through the gap between the boards and landed with a loud thud on the pine floor. He emitted a groan of pain.

"Try not to break the house, Jonas," his brother teased. "We are only borrowing it for one night."

"Just help me up!" Jonas retorted angrily.

Justus reached down and then pulled his brother to his feet. They stood quietly and peered into the blackness around them. It took a little while, but once their eyes adjusted to the darkness, they were able to survey their surroundings. A few pieces of furniture remained in the room. Otherwise, the little house was empty.

"What now?" asked Jonas.

Justus pointed to the large stone fireplace. "We build a fire and wait for Charity."

"Dare we build a fire? Someone might see us."

"We are so deep in the woods that no one could possibly see the light of the fire. Besides, if anyone does approach, we can easily make our escape out the back window." He smiled and then patted his little brother reassuringly on the shoulder. "We are safe here. Let us collect some wood and then I will build us a cheerful fire. I plan on sleeping warm tonight. I think we deserve a good, warm sleep."

"I saw an old piggin bucket on the back porch," Jonas declared. "I will go and fetch us some water from the creek."

"That sounds good," affirmed Justus. He teased, "But

try not to tear the house down as you are going and coming."

Jonas shook his fist playfully at his brother and then trudged toward the partially open window.

Less than an hour later, the boys had a roaring fire in the fireplace. They sat cross-legged in front of the blaze, sipping cool water and enjoying the comforting warmth. They chatted happily, told stories, laughed, and shared memories of their lives before indenture. It was good to be under a roof once again. Indeed, for a moment they almost forgot that they were runaway, homeless criminals.

A gentle tap on the door and a rattling of the iron lock brought their conversation to a sudden, frightened halt. Seconds later, the door swung open. A smiling Charity MacLellan stepped inside. She carried a basket in her left hand and a large bundle beneath her right arm.

Justus was thoroughly confused. "How did you open the lock?" he asked as he leapt to his feet. "It is solid iron!"

She sat her cargo down on the floor and then, smiling broadly, held up a huge key.

"Where on earth did you get that?" inquired Jonas, eyes wide in surprise.

Charity looked around the room and sighed. "This was once my home. My father built it with his own hands. It has been empty ever since my mother died. There is no deed that I am aware of, so technically no one owns it. Whoever claims or pays the taxes on this land will get ownership of the house. But, for now, no one seems to know about it. The homestead has been long forgotten. I have been taking care of the place for a couple of years now. I come here whenever I have the opportunity. I love this house. It is my own personal refuge. I placed the locks on the doors to keep vagrants out." She grinned. "But I see that you two vagabonds still found your way inside."

Jonas giggled and then pointed at her basket. "I smell something tasty. What's for supper?"

Charity picked up the basket and sauntered toward the fire. "I brought some leftover venison stew and a loaf of bread. But the stew will need to warm just a bit." She smiled and then added, "There might even be a slice or two of mulberry pie in my basket."

She removed a small iron pot from her basket, walked over to the fireplace, and hung the handle of the pot on the long arm of the fireplace crane. She used a stick to push the pot into the fireplace so that it was dangling over the glowing bed of coals.

"There!" she declared. "Soon you shall have a hot meal." She then fetched the linen bundle from beside the door. "I also brought you some clean clothes."

Charity opened the bundle. Inside were four white shirts, two well-worn but clean weskits, two pairs of wool breeches, and several pairs of linen stockings. Both boys' eyes widened in joy and surprise.

"Wherever did you get all of these fine clothes?" exclaimed Justus. He eyed her sternly. "You did not steal them, did you?"

Charity giggled at the thought. "No, I did not steal them. I wash all the laundry for the travelers who stay overnight in the upstairs rooms of the tavern. I also clean the bedchambers. Sometimes people forget things when they leave, so I keep any abandoned or unclaimed pieces of clothing. I mend anything that requires mending. Whenever I need some extra money of my own, I sell a garment or two at the town market for a few pence."

"But we cannot accept such a generous gift," Jonas objected. "You need that money."

"Yes, you can accept it ... and you shall. I insist. It is the very least that I can do."

"Then, we shall pay you for them," declared Justus as he dug into his weskit pocket to retrieve his coin purse. "*I* insist."

Charity placed both hands on her hips and glowered stormily at Justus. "You will do no such thing, Justus Avery! 'Tis an insult to offer payment for something given as a gift. Or didn't they teach you any manners on your Virginia plantation?"

Justus sighed. He returned the coin purse to his pocket. "No, Miss Charity. They taught me no such manners. But I assure you that, when I was a lad back in England, my mother and father did." He nodded gratefully. "We are most thankful for and humbled by your very generous gift."

She paused for a moment and stared at the handsome young man before her. He seemed completely honest. There was an innocence about him. She trusted him. In a way, she admired him. And she was determined to help him find his father.

Charity reached into the pocket of her apron. "I have something else for you." She handed a folded piece of paper to Justus.

"What is this?" he inquired softly.

"It is a map that will lead you all the way to Baltimore. I have plotted out the safest route for you. You will travel north through London Town, then cut northeast around the headwaters of the Patapsco River. You will go just south of New Town and then you will find Baltimore." She scowled. "But I do not think you will like it. It is a very loud, stinky, and unpleasant place."

Justus smiled warmly. "Well, we have no intentions of staying there for long, I assure you."

"Good!" Charity chirped as she turned and ambled to the fireplace. "Now, let us get a hot supper in you. While you eat, you can tell me more about yourselves. Then, you will need a good night's rest." She grinned happily and waved a wooden spoon playfully in their direction. "Because tomorrow the Avery lads are going to go and find their papa!"

5
BALTIMORE

Early Morning - Two Days Later

Justus and Jonas entered Baltimore shortly after dawn. Already the city was busy and bustling with activity. It was, as Charity had warned them, a very big, noisy, and smelly place. The boys were mesmerized by the size and scope of everything. The sheer number of human beings crammed into one location was overwhelming to the two young, innocent farm boys.

"These people look like bees swarming a honeycomb," marveled Jonas.

"More like maggots on a carcass," suggested Justus.

"I agree." Jonas shook his head. "I do not like this place."

He felt an elbow nudging his side. Justus was pointing down the street. Jonas gulped in disbelief. He watched in dismay as a man stepped out of a doorway with his chamber pot in hand and then poured the contents ... human toilet waste ... into the middle of the street. The fellow promptly returned the lid to his pot and then strolled, apparently quite satisfied with himself, back inside his house.

"Can you believe that?" gasped Jonas. "These people live like animals! How can they live in the middle of such filth?"

Justus gagged and shook his head in disgust. "Let's keep moving. The quicker we get out of this nasty place the better. But first we must find the hospital where they took Papa."

Jonas nodded determinedly. "I'm ready."

For the next several hours the boys scoured the various districts of Baltimore in search of the Almshouse Hospital and its surgeon, Dr. Thaddeus Hamilton. They inquired inside businesses, shops, and taverns throughout the city. But, to their dismay, no one they encountered had ever heard of the hospital *or* the doctor. Indeed, it seemed as if almost everyone they talked to was relatively new to Baltimore. By the time of the noon hour, the boys were thoroughly frustrated and heartbroken. Their only clue to their father's whereabouts, that faded message in the old glass bottle, was looking more and more like a dead end rather than an actual clue.

"I am famished. Let's get some food," Justus urged. "While we eat, perhaps we can come up with another plan. It seems clear that our current approach is not working."

Jonas nodded and grinned. "I can always eat."

The boys purchased some sliced salted ham and bread from a street vendor and then sought out a place to sit in the shade. They constructed sandwiches and soon were enjoying a leisurely dinner, munching on their food and sipping cool water from their canteens. All the while they amused themselves by watching the people of the bustling city as they scurried about and attended to their daily lives and business. It was a carnival of humanity unlike anything they had ever before witnessed.

"I've been thinking," Justus announced. "I believe we are wasting our time by simply roaming all over town and knocking on doors. This city is simply too large. It spreads outward for miles. We cannot search the entire city. It would take months ... years maybe."

"What, then, must we do differently?" Jonas asked.

"We need to go to a place that we have not yet visited ... the most obvious place, I think."

Curious, Jonas raised his eyebrows. "And where might that be?"

"We need to go down to the docks and the waterfront." He paused to let Jonas consider his idea. "Think about it. When the sailors took Papa from our ship, they would not have carried him very far. They would have gone to the nearest hospital, don't you think? So, this Almshouse Hospital *has* to be somewhere near the docks."

Jonas nodded slowly. His face erupted into a smile. "That makes sense to me."

Justus slapped his brother happily on the knee. "Good! Finish your sandwich and then let's go!"

LESS THAN AN HOUR LATER THE BOYS WERE WALKING along the docks at the port of Baltimore. The place was as they remembered it ... teeming with ships, wagons, sailors, deckhands, and dock workers. Much like Baltimore city, the waterfront was a place of feverish activity and commerce. After a few brief inquiries, the lads quickly located the office of the dock foreman. Justus bravely knocked on the front door.

A voice growled from inside, "What do you want? I'm busy!"

Justus and Jonas opened the door and then stepped timidly inside. The foreman was standing behind his desk. He was a lean, tanned fellow. He puffed on his clay pipe as he examined a long, wrinkled strip of yellowed parchment paper.

"Please excuse us for intruding," Justus declared, removing his cocked hat.

"What do you lads want? If you are looking for work, there are way far too many grown menfolk in line ahead of you. I have no work for children on *my* docks."

Justus gulped nervously. "No, sir. We are not looking for work. We are merely seeking information."

The man tossed the piece of paper onto his desk. He was clearly aggravated. "I am not in the information business. You boys are wasting my time. I must ask you to leave."

"Please, sir," Justus begged. "We are looking for a hospital that we believe must be located somewhere near these docks. Our father, who was injured on board ship a few years ago, was taken there. We became separated from him. Now we are trying to find him."

The man leaned forward and placed his knuckles on his desk. His eyes narrowed. "You boys are those runaway indentures, aren't you? Last name of Avery. You're from Frederick County in Virginia. I have seen papers posted all over town with your images on them."

A chill shot down Justus' spine. They had been discovered! Surely, this surly man was going to turn them in and claim Mr. Dawson's generous reward!

Justus took a deep breath and then nodded. "Yes, sir. We are Justus and Jonas Avery. We fled indentured servitude. That much is true. But, sir, you must understand that we were sold unjustly. We were removed from our father without his consent or knowledge."

The fellow turned and walked to the tiny window in the front of his office. He peered through the wavy glass toward the ships that lined the docks. He said nothing for a short while. After an agonizingly long period of silence, he turned and faced the boys and then crossed his arms.

"You were sold, no doubt, by that no-good Frenchman, Ichabod Rochelle." He turned his head to one side and spat angrily onto the rough wood floor.

Jonas glanced, confused, at his brother. A bead of nervous sweat trickled down Justus' brow.

"Yes ... yes, sir," stammered Justus. "He is the root of all our misery. He is the man who took all our family's property, stole us away, and then sold us to Mr. Benedict Dawson of Virginia."

The man's face displayed obvious disgust. "I know all about Captain Rochelle and his evil, thieving, inhuman ways. That man, if you can call him a man, is a scoundrel of the worst sort. He would sell his own mother if he thought he could make a shilling in profit. I suspected that he was involved in this mess the moment I saw one of those handbills." He paused. "Still, the handsome reward offered for your capture does seem a bit odd."

Justus shrugged, feigning ignorance. He dared not mention the possibility of his father holding a fortune in silver and gold coin. "We thought the same thing, sir.

Truth be told, we doubted that we would even be missed. We are only two among dozens of indenture servants and slaves on his plantation. But, if he is placing advertisements here in Baltimore, then Mr. Dawson must want us back pretty badly."

"Indeed," growled the foreman. He motioned to a bench beside his desk. "Sit, boys, and rest easy. You need not fear me. I shall not turn you in to Dawson and his men, no matter the size of the reward. I have no desire to encourage or support Rochelle's crooked business, nor anyone who associates with him." He walked to his desk chair and then sat down. "My name is Abner Jackson. I have lived in Baltimore my entire life. I know most of the people and businesses throughout this town. Now, tell me ... what is this information that you seek?"

Justus and Jonas sat down, greatly relieved by the man's friendly and helpful attitude. Justus explained, "We are looking for the hospital where the sailors took our father, Jeremiah Avery."

The man nodded his understanding. "And you assume the hospital records might lead you to his location."

"Yes, sir," Jonas stated. "Or at least give us a clue. And we have a doctor's name, as well."

The foreman grinned at the younger of the boys. It was the first time that he had heard Jonas speak since the brothers enter his office. "That is a fine clue, indeed. So, tell me, Mr. Avery ... what is the name of this mysterious hospital?"

"It is called the *Almshouse Hospital*," answered Jonas.

"The doctor's name was Thaddeus Hamilton," added Justus. "One of the sailors wrote the information down for us before they took him away."

"I see." Mr. Jackson frowned. "I am familiar with the *Almshouse Hospital* and know its location. Unfortunately, it will not be much help to you."

"Why so?" demanded Justus, confused.

"Because it is no longer in operation. That old hospital shut down two or three years ago."

Both boys' shoulders sank in defeat. Jonas stared at his brother. Tears filled his eyes. Mr. Jackson could see how disappointed they were in hearing his news.

"Still, lads, you must not lose heart. The building is only three blocks north of here, on Argyle Street, one block east of the intersection of Market and Fleet Streets." He grabbed a piece of paper and took his goose feather quill in hand. Dipping the pen into the ink, he began to scribble a message. "I will give you a letter of recommendation. You should go to the neighborhood near the hospital and make your inquiries there. If anyone gives you any difficulty, you can show them this letter penned by my own hand and bearing my seal. My name and reputation carry some weight down here near the waterfront."

"We are most grateful, Mr. Jackson," Justus declared humbly.

"'Tis my pleasure, Squire Avery. I pray with all sincerity that you will locate and reunite with your long-lost father." Mr. Jackson signed his name, then daubed a blob of hot wax below the signature. He picked up a bronze wax stamp from its tray and then pressed it down hard into the wax. His seal bore the shape of a sailing ship. He handed the letter to Jonas. "I hope this helps."

The grinning lad took the letter from the affable dock foreman. "I am sure it will. Thank you, Mr. Jackson."

"You are most welcome," answered Mr. Jackson. "Now,

away with the both of you. I have work to do. But you must be careful as you go. You should not draw any attention to yourselves. There are men in this city who would not hesitate to capture you and claim that handsome reward."

"As well we know it," remarked Justus. He grinned. "We will try not to stir up any trouble."

Both boys stood and approached Mr. Jackson's desk. He stood and then shook both of their hands. Without uttering another word, Justus and Jonas turned and headed toward the door.

THE AVERY BROTHERS LEANED AGAINST THE DUST-encrusted glass. They cupped their hands around their eyes to shield them from the bright sunlight so that they might see inside the dark room that was once the Almshouse Hospital. It was little more than a filthy, cluttered, neglected mess.

"It doesn't look like anyone has set foot in that room for years," remarked Jonas forlornly.

Justus groaned in frustration. He exclaimed, "Why does everything have to be so difficult for us?"

A deep, gravelly voice interrupted their conversation. "What are you boys doing over yonder? You have no business lurking around that old building. Get away from there!"

The Avery brothers turned and quickly spotted the source of the gruff voice. Across the street was a surly shop keeper. He was standing in the open doorway of his dry goods store. His arms were crossed and resting upon his exceptionally large, round belly.

"Come on," Justus whispered. "And let me do the talking." He immediately began walking toward the shopkeeper. Jonas followed closely behind.

Justus removed his cocked hat in a respectful gesture. "Begging your pardon, sir. We are attempting to find a long-lost relative who received treatment at the old *Almshouse Hospital*."

"Well, you're out of luck, I'm afraid. That old clinic closed down back in '72."

Justus nodded. "We heard about that." He reached into his pocket and removed the letter penned by Mr. Jackson, the dock foreman. "Mr. Jackson, the boss down at the docks, sent us over here to make inquiries."

The shopkeeper's face registered surprise. "Abner Jackson sent you?"

Justus nodded. "Yes, sir. He gave us this letter of support."

He handed the note to the fellow and waited as the man scanned the words. He seemed impressed that they carried the dock foreman's correspondence. He quickly handed the letter back to Justus.

"Well, like I said ... the hospital closed three years ago this past winter."

"And what of Dr. Thaddeus Hamilton?" asked Jonas.

The shopkeeper emitted a sarcastic laugh. "Thad Hamilton? He was no doctor; I can assure you. I knew that boy all my life. He and I grew up together. He was nothing but a self-proclaimed sawbones. It was the craziest thing! One day, he just up and declared himself to be a surgeon! That was about twenty years ago, back when he started that God-awful hospital. And you must understand ... it was a horrible, death-filled place. Only the poorest of the poor went to him for medical help. Everyone else knew better." The man chuckled. "The good Lord did this city a favor when Thad caught that fever and died. No doubt many lives were spared because of it." He nodded toward the empty hospital building. "That's why the place closed down, you know. When Thad died the hospital died with him. Good riddance, if you ask me."

The boys were instantly heartbroken by the news. The shopkeeper could not help but see their disappointment.

"I am truly sorry, lads. I hate to be the bearer of such bad news. I wish that I could be of more help to you."

Justus nodded respectfully. "Thank you, anyway, sir. We bid you a kind farewell."

Dejected, Justus and Jonas turned to walk away.

"Wait, boys!" The man stepped out of the doorway and into the muddy street. "I do not know if it will be of any help to you, at all, but old Thad did keep some papers and journals from his work."

Instantly, Justus' spirits lifted. He turned and approached the shopkeeper excitedly. "What happened to them? Do you know where those documents are now stored?"

"As I understand it, all of his records were transferred to the *Baltimore County and Town Almshouse*. It is located six blocks north and three blocks west of here. Everyone knows the location. It is where all the poor folk of Baltimore go for their doctoring."

"Thank you, sir!" exclaimed Justus excitedly. "Thank you very, very much!"

"You're most welcome." The fellow turned to walk back into his store. He called over his shoulder, "Good luck to you."

Justus and Jonas turned and immediately sprinted down the street to go in search of the other hospital. There could be records there. It was a crucial clue. Finally, they were making some progress!

"I SIMPLY CANNOT ALLOW CHILDREN FROM OFF THE street to examine the official records of this hospital!" exclaimed the woman seated behind the desk. "Your request is both absurd and inappropriate!"

Justus exhaled in frustration. "Madam, as I have already explained, we do not wish to see the records of *this* hospital. We are looking for our father, who was treated at the old *Almshouse Hospital* down near the docks. The records we seek are from over five years ago. A shopkeeper told us that Dr. Hamilton's records were all transferred here, to this hospital. We hope that some of his papers may provide us with a clue to our father's location. We simply need to have a look at Dr. Hamilton's old logbooks."

The woman closed her eyes and shook her head emphatically. "I cannot allow you to inspect *those* documents, either."

He reached into his pocket and retrieved the letter from Mr. Jackson. "Please, Madam. Just allow us to have a quick look. We have a letter of reference to vouch for our sincerity."

The woman waved her hand dismissively in Justus' face. "You may keep your letter. It holds no sway with me. I simply will not allow you access to our files. Now, go! Get out of here now, or I will be forced to fetch the constable."

Justus gazed at the woman with steely, angry eyes. "That is your final decision, then?"

"Yes! I have said it thrice already!" She stood and then pointed at the front door. "Now, go! Do not make me say *that* again!"

As Justus tucked the letter back into his pocket, Jonas tugged gently at his arm.

"Come on, Justus. 'Tis useless to hope for any help from this wicked, heartless old crone."

"Old crone?" echoed the woman, her face reddening in anger and offense.

"That is what he said," retorted Justus spitefully. "Do not make him say it *again*!"

The Avery brothers turned and then stormed out of the hospital. Jonas slammed the door angrily behind them.

"Well, I guess that's it," declared Jonas. "Thaddeus Hamilton's records are beyond our reach."

"Perhaps not," Justus replied, winking.

"What do you mean?" Jonas' face expanded into a huge smile. "You have a plan, don't you?"

Justus shrugged. "The front door during broad daylight isn't the only way into that big building. There has to be a back door, as well."

"Or a window ..." added Jonas, grinning mischievously. "We both know how to squeeze through a window if needs be. Right?"

Justus nodded. "Right. We shall just have to find us

another way in." He glanced at the sky. "It will be dark in a couple of hours. Let's go find an inexpensive tavern, get us a hot meal, and rent a bed for the night. Then, we can come back later ... after Baltimore has gone to sleep."

6
A CLUE

1:00 AM

Justus and Jonas huddled for a quick conference in the dark alleyway. They concealed themselves behind a large wooden crate. Both boys were beyond frustrated. They had been searching for over an hour for a way into the hospital. So far all of their efforts had failed.

"This hospital is locked up tight as a jailhouse!" hissed Jonas angrily. "Every door is locked. Every window is nailed shut. There are even iron bars on the windows. Why?"

Justus shrugged. "It is not the safest part of town, that much is certain." He smiled mischievously. "I reckon that we are not the only criminals who ever attempted to sneak into this place."

Jonas nodded. "You're probably right. But what will we do now? It's getting late. Should we give up and head on back to our room?"

Justus glanced left and right along the alleyway. He

shook his head. "No, I'm not ready to give up just yet. Let's try once more. If we still can't find any place to get in, then we will stop for the night and come back tomorrow for another look in the daylight. Then, maybe, we can try again tomorrow night."

"You truly want to spend another night in this awful city?" whined Jonas dejectedly.

"I don't *want* to. But if that is what it takes to find Papa, then I am most certainly willing to do so. Come on. We have talked long enough. It is time for action."

The boys slithered from behind the crate and then crept down the alleyway that ran alongside the hospital building. The flame of a faraway streetlamp filled the dark alley with a dull yellow glow. They hugged close against the wall, careful to remain hidden in the shadows. As they were nearing the rear corner of the building Justus stepped on something. He heard a hollow, metallic clang. It felt odd ... almost as if something had shifted beneath his foot.

"Hold on!" he hissed. "I think we may have discovered something." He stopped, knelt down, and then felt the area around his feet.

"What is it?" whispered Jonas.

"It is some kind of iron plate. It is pretty big." Justus ran his fingers along the edge of the iron plate until they touched the brick of the building. "I am not certain, but I think this may be the place where they bring in firewood."

"Firewood? In the basement?" asked Jonas, confused.

"It is how they do things in the city. If I am right, there is a hole beneath this slab of iron. The men who operate the wood wagon drive their rig into the alley, move the plate aside, drop the wood in, and then cover it back up when they are done. All of the wood for a building like this one is kept underground and in the dry. Whenever they need wood for the fireplaces, they just send someone down to fetch it. It's brilliant, actually. They need not go outside into the cold weather to get their wood."

"But they probably have a crew of grown men when they deliver firewood." He knelt down and felt the iron plate. "This thing is very large and sure to be heavy. Do you truly think *we* can move it?"

Justus nodded. "I believe we can. We are both strong lads. Hopefully the hole beneath will be big enough for us to get inside."

"Then, do you think we have found our way in?" Jonas asked, his voice filled with hope.

"Perhaps. There is only one way to find out. Help me move this thing."

The boys gripped the iron cover along one edge and then, on a count of three, gave it a mighty shove. There was a loud scraping sound as the iron grinded against brick and stone. The plate shifted sideways, exposing a two-foot-wide hole that opened into the building's basement. Even though it was very dark, they could still see a large pile of firewood below.

Justus nudged his brother happily. "I *was* right! This is definitely how we are going to get in! Let's go. We don't have all night."

He went through the opening without hesitation and dropped nimbly onto the mountainous woodpile. He landed on his feet, quickly scooted out of the way, and then whispered, "Come on! It's your turn."

Jonas dropped his legs through the hole and then slowly squeezed the rest of his body through. He hesitated, dangling from the ledge by his fingertips.

"Just let go!" urged Justus, growing impatient. "The wood is only about three feet below your shoes. You'll be fine."

Jonas took a deep breath as he mustered the courage to release his grip. Finally, he let go. His descent into the basement was not as nimble or effortless as was his older brother's. He dropped awkwardly, his body twisting sideways in mid-air. He landed on his side atop the woodpile. The sudden impact knocked the wind out of him. He gasped as he fought for a breath. He lay on his side for a moment and eventually calmed himself. It was not long before his breathing returned. Slowly and carefully, he rolled over onto his knees.

"That was ugly. I think I felt the entire woodpile shift," teased Justus, smiling. "Come on. Let's get moving."

The brothers crawled carefully across the top of the woodpile. Jagged pieces of wood and tiny, needle-like splinters dug into their skin. It took several seconds for them to reach the edge and then climb down from the pile. By that time their eyes had adjusted to the darkness in the basement.

"Seriously, are you all right?" asked Justus. "You landed pretty hard."

Jonas nodded. "Nothing was hurt but my pride." He turned and stared at the enormous woodpile and the uncovered hole high above. "Brother, I don't think we can climb all the way back up there. That hole is way too high for me to reach. How will we ever get out of here?"

Justus grinned. "We will walk out the front door, of course."

Jonas chuckled. "I hadn't thought of that. I suppose locks are intended to keep people out, not keep people in.

So, then we have a plan. We will exit through the front door. But where do you think they keep the old records and papers?"

Justus replied, "Right before that old lady tossed us out today, I noticed a sign on the wall in the lobby. It said that *'Library and Records'* were on the second floor."

Jonas grinned excitedly. "That must be the place, then. Let's go and find the clue that will lead us to Papa!"

Justus and Jonas immediately made their way toward a door at the far end of the room. Since it was the only exit from the basement, the boys assumed that it led to a stairway. When they reached it, Justus paused, turned to his brother, and lifted his finger to his lips.

He whispered, "Keep absolutely quiet!"

Jonas nodded. Slowly, Justus reached for the doorknob and then gave it a silent turn. He opened the door slightly and then peeked through. On the other side of the door was a dark, narrow stairway that ascended to the first floor. There was a wide gap beneath the door at the top of the stairs. The boys could see the dull glow of candlelight through the gap.

"All clear," Justus whispered over his shoulder.

The boys moved as stealthily as they could up the creaky stairway. Once they reached the top, they lay down and peered through the crack beneath the door. They observed in silence for several minutes. Thankfully, they saw no movement.

Justus leaned close to his brother's ear and whispered, "As I recall, the stairway to the second floor is right next to this one. It should be to our left. I will take the lead. Follow me and stay close."

Jonas gave his brother a silent "thumbs up." Justus rose,

quietly cracked the door open, and then slithered through the gap. Jonas followed. Justus darted left to the door that led to the second-floor stairway. Without making any sound at all, he opened the door and then stepped inside. Jonas, right behind him, pulled the heavy oak door closed. They paused at the bottom of yet another flight of stairs.

"That was almost too easy," Jonas whispered.

"The easy part is over, I fear," Justus warned forebodingly. "I expected the first floor to be empty." He pointed up the stairs. "But there will likely be people up there on the second floor. No doubt, sick patients are asleep in their beds. And there are probably some maids and other night attendants. This is where things may get tricky."

"We can do it," Jonas whispered confidently.

Justus nodded. "Let's just find what we are looking for and then get out of here."

"Agreed," responded Jonas.

Without speaking another word, the brothers quietly ascended the narrow stairs. They reached the top quickly and then, as they had done before, lay low against the floor to observe through the crack beneath the door. Then, quite unexpectedly, someone wearing white linen stockings glided silently past the door barely two feet from the boys' faces. Jonas was so startled by the surprising sight that he recoiled and almost tumbled backwards down the stairs. Justus had to grab his shoulder to steady him.

"It was only one of the lady attendants," Justus whispered. "She is just doing her job."

"But why is she walking around at night in her stocking feet? Why no shoes?" He removed his hat and wiped a bead of nervous sweat from his brow. "I thought it was a ghost! Those stocking feet scared the life out of me. I never heard them. I only saw them."

"Shoes make noise, especially in the silence of night. I imagine all the workers go about in their stocking feet at night, so they do not disturb the sleeping patients."

Jonas was still trembling. He nodded. "I suppose that makes sense."

They watched for a while longer. They saw no one else. Justus patted his brother on the arm. "It is time to make a move. But only one of us should go on from here. Together we might make too much noise and risk getting caught. I will go and search for the documents that we seek. You stay here and keep watch. If you are discovered, you must sound an alarm."

"Sound an alarm?" whispered Jonas, confused.

Justus nodded. "Make lots of noise and scream, '*Fire!*' Shout madly and urge everyone to get out of the building. Scream as loudly as you can. Wake everyone in the building. We can make our escape in the confusion." He removed his cocked hat and handed it to his brother. Next, he unlatched the buckles on his black leather shoes. He removed the shoes and placed them against the wall.

"You're going in your stocking feet, too, eh?"

Justus nodded. "Stealth is our best weapon." He knelt in front of the door and took hold of the knob. He glanced over his shoulder at his little brother. "I will be back soon. Don't get in any trouble while I'm gone."

Jonas smiled and countered, "Don't get caught."

"I won't. I promise."

Justus turned the doorknob slowly. There was a dull, muffled click. He opened the door just wide enough for his head to fit through the crack. He scanned left and right.

No one was in the hallway. He crawled without hesitation through the narrow opening, closed the door silently behind him, and then darted to the far side of the hall. He concealed himself in the shadows behind a small desk. He was absolutely terrified and could feel his heart pounding inside his chest. He rested for a moment as he attempted to calm himself and control his breathing.

After a short rest, he peeked around the corner of the desk and stole a glance in each direction. Seeing no one, he crouched low and then crept down the hall. He passed by three ward rooms. He peeked through the glass panes in each door. Inside each ward there was a single female nursing attendant keeping watch over her slumbering patients. The women were each seated at small, candle-illuminated desks. Two of them were doing paperwork. One, an older-looking woman, appeared to be dozing.

Justus crept past the patient wards and continued on his silent mission. At long last he reached the room that was the object of his search. It was at the far end of the hallway. The door was marked with a sign that read, *'Library and Records.'* He crawled to the doorway, reached up, and then grasped the doorknob. He gave it a gentle turn. The mechanism clicked and the door opened slightly. He could not believe his luck! The library door was not locked!

He whispered to himself victoriously, "*Now I will find the truth!*"

He opened the door just wide enough to enter and then, once through, quietly closed it behind him. He paused for a moment to allow his eyes to adjust to the darkness inside the library. The only illumination was pale moonlight mixed with a yellow glow from the street lanterns outside the window. Justus went to the window and pulled back the curtain to allow in more light from the street lanterns.

The tiny library was sparsely furnished. It contained two fold-top secretary desks and two long wooden cabinets. Along one wall there was a set of tall shelves that contained dozens of leather-bound books.

Justus did not even know where to begin his search. He tried to imagine where the old *Almshouse Hospital* records might be kept. His first notion was to check the wooden cabinets. He moved to the first cabinet. It was locked tight with a heavy iron padlock. He checked the second cabinet. It, too, was secured with an iron lock.

"*These probably contain the records of this hospital*," he thought. "*Why else would they be locked?*" He sighed, frustrated, and prayed that the old *Almshouse Hospital* records were not contained within those locked boxes. If so, then he would never see them.

Frustrated, he turned his attention to the bookshelves. He spotted a small folding ladder leaning against a nearby wall. He assumed that the office workers used it to retrieve books from the higher shelves. He fetched the ladder and unfolded it. He would need it to reach the very top shelves.

"*I will work from left to right, top to bottom, and check every book*," he declared to himself.

Justus worked quickly. The upper shelves contained what appeared to be medical books and reference texts. They were all professionally printed, published volumes and of no interest to him. The longer he searched the more dejected he became. He was not at all interested in surveying a medical library. He needed to find a handwritten record ... a journal or logbook of some sort.

He systematically checked every shelf. His frustration and disappointment grew as he progressed. He was also aware of how painfully long his search was taking. No doubt Jonas was out of his mind with worry and wondering what was taking him so long. Determined, he searched on. He was on the verge of giving up when, on the very bottom shelf, he spotted a thick, black, dust-encrusted book. There was a single, faded word on the spine. It simply said, "*Almshouse.*"

Justus' heart skipped a beat. With trembling fingers, he removed the book from the shelf and opened the cover. Unlike all of the other books he had checked, this one did not contain printed words. Instead, it had words written in quill and ink. The first page identified the owner of the book. It read, *'Thaddeus Hamilton, Surgeon.'*

"I've found it!" Justus whispered excitedly, raising a silent fist in victory.

He carried the book to the window so that he might have more light to see. He scanned the first few pages. There were dates for each entry, along with a name, diagnosis, and, finally, the medical outcome of each patient. Tragically, most entries ended with the word *'Deceased.'*

Justus shook his head and thought, "*There can be no doubt. Thaddeus Hamilton was a dreadful doctor.*"

He flipped through the pages until he reached the month of May, 1770. Justus gasped when he spotted his father's name. His entry covered an entire page in the notebook. Justus did not read the words. There was no time. It was urgent that he make his escape.

Without hesitation he carefully tore the page from the journal, folded it, and then tucked it inside the pocket of his coat. Before he left the room, he worked to erase any evidence of his having been there. He returned the book to its proper place on the shelf. He returned to ladder to the spot where it had been stored. Finally, he pulled the curtain closed. He scanned the room to make sure that he had not left anything out of place. Satisfied, he readied himself to depart.

Slowly, silently, Justus turned the knob and cracked the door. He poked his head through the opening, listened, and watched for several seconds before stepping out into the hallway. The building was silent. He saw no movement. Quick as a flash, he darted down the long hallway toward the staircase door. Once there, he opened it, stepped onto the top stair, and then instantly closed the door behind him.

"Did you find it?" Jonas hissed excitedly.

Justus nodded, smiling. "I found it."

Jonas grinned happily. "What did it say?"

"I do not know," confessed Justus. "I tore out the page that contained Father's information. We will go back to our room and read it there. Right now, though, let's get out of here before we get caught. I don't want to spend the rest of the night in jail."

Quickly, Justus donned his shoes and hat. The brothers scurried down the steps, tore through the door, and then sprinted through the first-floor lobby. Moments later they were out the front door and running down the street toward their boarding house.

THE EXHAUSTED BOYS QUIETLY CLIMBED THE STAIRS TO their sleeping chamber. When Jonas lifted the latch and opened the door they were greeted by a chorus of snores. Though they had been the only ones assigned to the room earlier in the evening, now it was filled to capacity. At least a dozen men occupied the cots and sleeping mats inside the stuffy, stinky, crowded room.

"I thought we had the place to ourselves! Where did all these men come from?" hissed Jonas, disappointment filling his voice.

"They must have arrived late in the evening, while we were out."

Suddenly, Jonas gagged. He instantly closed the door and then turned to face his brother. He pinched his nose closed between his thumb and forefinger. He declared, "I'm not sleeping in there! Did you get a whiff of that smell? That room smells like an outhouse ... one with a dead rat in it!"

"I smelled it," replied Justus, shaking his head in disgust. "I'll not set foot in that room, either." He shrugged. "Oh, well ... there goes a sixpence, I reckon."

"They can keep the money," declared Jonas, still gagging. "Let's go back downstairs. We can light some candles in the dining hall and examine the paper there. When we're done, we can stoke the fire and make us a mat beside the hearth."

Justus nodded. "Good idea." He grinned. "We've definitely slept in worse places."

They turned without delay and headed back downstairs to the dining hall. Justus retrieved two candle stands from the mantle and lit both candles from the withering fire in the fireplace. While he was doing that Jonas fetched them each a mug of cold milk from the serving kitchen. Seconds later they were seated side-by-side at one of the dining tables. Justus reached a trembling hand into his coat pocket and retrieved the page that he had taken from the book. He unfolded the paper and placed it on the table between the two candles.

"Taking that page from the book was excellent thinking," said Jonas. "They will never even know it is gone."

"True. I doubt that the book has been touched since it was placed on the shelf. It was completely covered in dust. No one cares about those old records."

"No one but that nasty old crone who turned us away." Jonas chuckled and then nudged his older brother with his elbow. "Well, let's get on with it. I want to know what happened to our Papa."

Justus nodded. He cleared his throat and then read the words aloud.

Jeremiah Avery, Immigrant - England

Arrived Port of Baltimore, 6 May 1770. Patient brought to hospital by fellow sailors. Mr. Avery was, according to them, a passenger who was drafted into the crew after the tragic loss of numerous crewmen at sea. Wife died during journey. Possessions inventoried: One Bible, one cobbler's case with tools, one trunk containing personal clothing & sundries. Purse contains fifty cents in Spanish silver.

Injuries and Initial Treatment – Injury occurred from a fall from the ship's mast. Both legs broken below knees. Cut on forehead. Unconscious. Bones set and legs boarded and wrapped. Cut stitched and dressed.

Updates:

17 May 1770 – Patient has regained consciousness. Experi-

encing severe loss of memory. Knows his name, profession (cobbler), and former home. Has no memories of sea voyage. Has asked many questions about his family. I have informed him that he arrived alone and that his family likely died at sea.

23 July 1770 – Patient recovering well physically. However, mental status is lagging. Patient's grief for loss of family remains severe. Monetary expenses for care, medicine, and food are mounting. Since patient is without financial resources, I must seek relief from county court.

18 August 1770 – J. Avery declared destitute by county judge and placed into servitude for nonpayment of medical debt in excess of fifteen pounds sterling. Indenture filed in my name.

21 August 1770 – Patient able to walk with use of crutches. Discharged. Indenture sold to E. Magnusson, Cobbler of Baltimore City.

Justus flipped the page over. There was nothing on the back. "That is all." He turned slowly to face his brother. "Papa was sold, too. He is now an indentured servant." A single tear trickled down his cheek. "And he believes we are dead."

Jonas was confused. "But I do not understand. Why could he not pay for his care? He had plenty of money. He carried all of his life savings."

"Perhaps Captain Rochelle took it," Justus suggested.

Jonas shook his head. "No. Don't you remember when we overheard Sledge back at the bear's den? He had recently seen a letter from Captain Rochelle. It's been five years, yet both of them are still trying to get their hands on Papa's money."

Justus nodded in agreement. "You're right. That letter proves they haven't found him or his treasure yet. So, *we* must beat them to it." He paused. "Maybe Papa could not remember where he hid his silver and gold. That is why he could not pay his hospital bill. The records did say he suffered from loss of memory."

Jonas nodded. "That would explain a lot." He sighed. "All right ... so what do we do now?"

Justus picked up the journal page from the table and smiled victoriously. "We have something that Captain Rochelle and Mr. Dawson do not have. We have a clue!"

"Right!" affirmed Jonas smiling. "Now all we need to do is find this cobbler." He glanced at the page again. "We must track down this fellow, '*Mr. E. Magnusson*.'"

7
THE POTTER

The Next Morning

Justus and Jonas stood at a busy intersection near the boarding house. From that one spot they could see several signs indicating the presence of shoe or cobbler shops.

"Shoes! Shoes! Everywhere, shoes! How can there be so many shoemakers and cobblers in one city?" complained Jonas. "Just look at all those signs!" He crossed his arms and pouted. "And this is only one city block. Just imagine how many more there must be in all of Baltimore. How can we possibly find one fellow amongst them all?"

Justus reassured him calmly, "We will follow the same strategy as we did when we were looking for the *Almshouse Hospital*. We assumed that the hospital was close to the docks, and we were correct. Right?"

Jonas nodded reluctantly.

"Likewise, I think we can also assume that Mr. Magnusson's shop was someplace close to the hospital. It stands to reason that the doctor would have conducted business with someone he already knew. I'll bet Magnusson's shop is very near to the old hospital."

Jonas appeared slightly less frustrated. "That is good thinking. You may be right." He nodded. "All right, then ... where do we go first?"

"We go to the former site of the *Almshouse Hospital*, explore the streets around it, and then expand our search from there. We will go door-to-door. We'll split up so that we can cover more ground. I want us to find what we're looking for and then get out of this city." He glanced left and right and then frowned. "There are simply too many people here. I want to find Papa and then leave this place ... find us a nice, quiet spot somewhere in the country."

"Amen to that, Brother," said Jonas. He smiled, somewhat encouraged. "Let's get going."

Shortly After Noon

IT WAS A BUSY WORKDAY IN THE CITY OF BALTIMORE. The streets, as always, were crowded with people. Justus was leaning against a hitching rail in front of a small tavern and waiting for his brother. He was passing the time by whittling a stick with his pocketknife. Justus needed the mindless distraction. He was tired, frustrated, and discouraged. He had been searching for almost four hours and had not located a single soul who had ever heard of a man named Magnusson. Deep in his heart he was beginning to wonder if they would ever find him.

The tavern where he waited was their pre-determined

meeting point. Their plan was to meet there at the noon hour, purchase a hot meal, compare notes, and strategize. Jonas was a little late, but Justus did not feel any need to worry over him. His younger brother gave little thought to punctuality. No doubt he would arrive soon.

Suddenly, Justus heard his name shouted over the busy din of the crowded street. He instantly recognized his brother's high-pitched voice. He scanned the street for a glimpse of Jonas. He soon spotted him about a half-block to the east. The lad had climbed up onto a lamppost and was waving frantically at him. He was also grinning happily. He motioned with his hand for Justus to come to him. Justus folded his penny knife, tucked it into his haversack, and then took off running down the street. He reached his little brother quickly.

"What is it? Did you find something?"

Jonas nodded proudly. "I met a lady who remembers Mr. Magnusson."

"Where? Who?"

Jonas pointed down the street behind him. "Two streets west of here. She is an old lady who rents a room above a dry goods store. I met her as she was coming down the stairs from her room. She said she remembered Mr. Magnusson well, and that he was an excellent cobbler. But she also said that she has neither seen nor spoken to him for many years."

"Still, it is a good, solid clue. What about his shop?" Justus asked, growing excited. "Does she know where it is?"

"She said his shop is somewhere on Granby Street, three blocks north and five blocks west of here. She described his sign for me. She said it was a black shoe with the heel separated and dangling from it on a small piece of rope. It is marked, *'The Shoe Doctor.'* Pretty clever if you ask me."

"Well, what are we waiting for?" exclaimed Justus. "Let's go!"

❧

"I DON'T SEE THE SIGN," CONFESSED JUSTUS. HE WAS more frustrated than ever. "Are you certain this is the right place?"

"This is the street that the old lady told me about. That's all I know." Jonas sighed and then glanced at his brother. "I knew it sounded too easy. Like you said before ... nothing comes easy for us, does it?"

"No, it doesn't," agreed his older brother, frowning.

"What should we do now?" asked Jonas.

"We must go shop to shop and inquire. If a cobbler named Magnusson was ever here, then someone on Granby Street must know something. We will work this entire block. If we do not find anything here, we will check the blocks to the east and west."

"What about dinner?" asked Jonas. "We were planning to eat at the tavern, remember? I'm hungry."

Justus grinned. "You're always hungry. Forget about your belly for once and focus on the job at hand. We will enjoy an early supper *after* we find Mr. Magnusson."

Jonas frowned. "All right, then. Where do we begin?"

Justus pointed to a leather shop on a nearby corner. "We start at that first shop on the nearest corner and then work our way up that side. When we reach the end of the block, we will cross the street and come back down the other side. Sound good?"

"It sounds like a lot of talking to folks I don't know," grumbled Jonas unhappily. "And you know I don't like talking to strangers."

Two Hours Later

"HOW CAN EVERYONE BE NEW TO THIS TOWN?" complained Jonas. "Nary a shop on this block has been in operation for more than a year or two."

Justus shrugged. "It is how things are here, I suppose. Baltimore is a port city. Dozens of ships arrive every day. Thousands of immigrants have come to America through the port. Just remember, Jonas, only a few years ago we were amongst them."

"Well, I still do not like the city," retorted Jonas. "It is crowded, noisy, and stinky. I have decided once and for all ... I prefer the country."

"As do I." Justus grinned teasingly. "So, then, are you ready to head on back to the Dawson plantation and finish out your indenture?"

Jonas cut him a displeased, sideways glare. "I didn't say that."

"Good. I was just making sure. Then let us get back to our search." Justus pointed to a corner building. The sign hanging out front featured an image of a bowl and said, *'A. Denkins – Potter.'* "This is the last shop on the block. Let's check it and then move east to the next block."

"Or maybe we can find that early supper you promised me? My innards are rumbling."

Justus smiled. "Perhaps. I know how disagreeable you can become when you are hungry."

They walked to the door of the pottery shop and then entered, removing their hats as they stepped inside. A tiny bell over the door jingled, announcing their arrival. The shop was empty of people. The boys surveyed the room. Shelves lined the walls, all of them covered with beautifully glazed plates, bowls, and cups. Many of them had intricate and colorful designs. There was a small table near the door that held a variety of clay smoking pipes. Near the pipes was an assortment of fragrant tobaccos. It was a lovely and interesting shop. It was clear that the potter was very skilled in his craft.

"Hello!" called Justus. "Is anyone in the store?"

A lady called out from the back room, "I'll be with you in just a bit! I need to wash!"

A short time later a lovely young woman stepped through the open doorway in the rear of the shop. She was dressed in a gray gown and petticoat. She wore a protective apron over her clothing and a workman's cap on her head. Her hands and forearms were wet and dripping. There were streaks of gray-brown clay on her arms. Clearly, she was the artist behind all of the impressive pottery.

"Hello, lads," she greeted them, smiling. "Please pardon my unkempt appearance. I am Mrs. Abigail Denkins. How may I help you?"

"Greetings, Mrs. Denkins," responded Justus. "Do you run this shop?"

"Ordinarily my husband runs things here in the shop

whilst I work out back. I am the potter, you know. This morning, however, he had to step out for a while. That leaves me in charge of both the shop *and* the pottery-making." She lifted her arms. "It is not an easy task for a lady who is always up to her elbows in wet clay." She wiped a bead of sweat from her brow against the sleeve on her upper arm. "So, what can I get for you lads? Has your mother sent you in search of plates or bowls? A serving platter, perhaps?"

Justus smiled politely. "No, ma'am, we do not need any pottery. I am Justus Avery, and this is my brother, Jonas. We are looking for a cobbler by the name of Magnusson. We were told that he once operated a shop somewhere on this street. Have you heard of him or his shop?"

She nodded. "Aye. You are standing in it. This was Edward Magnusson's place. I'm told he operated a shoe repair on this corner for twenty years or more."

"Hallelujah!" exclaimed Jonas, dancing a jig. "We have found him at last! Now I get to eat!"

The woman stared at the lad, thoroughly confused.

"Where is Mr. Magnusson now?" asked Justus, ignoring his brother. "We *must* speak to him. It is a very urgent matter."

Mrs. Denkins frowned. "I am truly sorry to be the one to tell you, but Edward Magnusson died about two years ago. We bought the building from his nephew shortly after. The young fellow inherited all of his properties, but he is not a cobbler and had no interest in keeping a shoe shop. He is a lawyer up in Philadelphia and was only interested in the old man's money."

The boys were crestfallen. Edward Magnusson had been their only clue ... their only connection to their long-lost father. But he was dead and likely, the clue had died with him.

Jonas seemed on the verge of tears. He groaned, "Oh, Justus, we shall never find Papa now."

Mrs. Denkins appeared even more confused. "Was Edward Magnusson your father? I thought you said your name was Avery."

Justus shook his head. "No, ma'am. Mr. Magnusson owned our father's indenture." He sighed. "It is a long story and entirely too long to tell, I'm afraid."

"How long ago were you separated from him ... from your father, I mean?" she asked, suddenly curious.

"Five years ago," Justus answered.

Mrs. Denkins gasped. "But you are both such young lads! How? Why?"

Justus shook his head. "As I said before, our story is much too long to tell. And we have already taken enough of your time. We thank you, ma'am." He nudged his brother. "Let's go." He and Jonas turned to leave.

"Wait!" commanded the woman sternly.

The boys turned to face her. Their eyes were hollow and sad. She searched them for any hint of deception but saw none. It was clear that these two boys were quite sincere. She was instantly intrigued. She cut a glance at Jonas. The anguish that filled the young boy's face melted her heart. She decided immediately that she wanted to hear their story, no matter how long it might be.

"You boys are not going anywhere," she declared resolutely.

She walked to the door, bolted it, and then placed a sign in the window that said, *'Closed for Tea.'* She turned to the lads and rested her fists upon her hips.

"I am going upstairs to boil water for tea. You are going to join me there and explain to me what is going on. I *must* know everything."

One Hour Later

MRS. DENKINS SHOOK HER HEAD IN DISBELIEF. HER EYES were wide with wonder and shock and rimmed with tears. "What an incredible story! So, you lads escaped your indenture and have been on the run for almost two weeks now. Tell me, is that horrible man and his pack of hounds still pursuing you?"

Justus nodded. "So far as we know. Mr. Sledge is a determined man and not one to give up easily. He aims to catch us."

"The part about your hiding out in the bear's den was simply astounding. You are two very smart and cunning lads." She took a sip of her tea. "And you believe this entire conspiracy centers upon you father and his money?"

"Yes ma'am," Jonas responded. "As we understand it, everyone believes him to be in possession of an untold treasure of silver and gold." He frowned. "We simply want to find our father. We care nothing of any treasure."

They heard a door open below. It sounded like it came from the rear of the shop. They heard movement throughout the downstairs. Then a man called out, "Abigail! Where are you, dear? Why is the shop closed?"

"I am upstairs, Husband," she responded. "We have guests."

They heard the dull thud of footfalls on the staircase.

Seconds later a young, handsome gentleman appeared in the doorway at the top of the stairs. He seemed surprised when he discovered his wife seated at their dining table with two teen-aged boys. All three had teacups in front of them. There was a plate in the center of the table that held the remnants of a serving of sweet biscuits.

"What's this?" he inquired, one eyebrow raised. "Why have you closed the shop for tea with these lads?"

Mrs. Denkins stood. "Boys, this is my husband, Garner Denkins. Darling, this is Justus and Jonas Avery. They are brothers who have suffered a grave injustice and are now caught up in a grand search for their long-lost father."

Justus and Jonas stood and nodded respectfully to the master of the house.

"I am pleased to meet you, sir," declared Justus. "Your wife has been most kind to us. We are very grateful."

Mr. Denkins returned the nod. He still looked confused. "But what brings you here to *our* shop?"

Justus explained, "We came here in search of Mr. Edward Magnusson, the cobbler who once owned this building. He was the only link to our father that we have been able to find. But, alas, Mrs. Denkins has informed us of his death. Now I do not know what we are going to do. I do not know where we will look next."

"What was your father's connection to Mr. Magnusson?" inquired the man. "Were they business partners?"

Jonas shook his head. "No, sir. Our father was indentured to him."

The man frowned. "Indentured, you say? What about you? Were you indentured, as well?"

Justus nodded. "We were. Technically, we still are. But we recently fled our master."

He glared angrily at his wife. "Why, my dear, are you entertaining runaways and outlaws in our home?"

"You must hear them out, Garner," Abigail pleaded, taking her husband by the arm. "It is a grand and tragic tale. Their mother died and their father was injured on the journey to America. As a result, they became separated from him. The boys were then stolen from their father by a crooked sea captain and then sold into servitude. Later, their father was also sold into servitude because of his enormous medical bills. Now they are on a quest to reunite with him. Isn't it a moving tale?"

The man's face clouded with a mixture of anger and disgust. He turned to the boys. "The sea captain who sold you into servitude ... his name wouldn't happen to be Rochelle, would it?"

Justus' eyes widened in surprise. "Yes, sir. Ichabod Rochelle. Have you heard of him?"

The man scowled. "Everyone in Baltimore has heard of Ichabod Rochelle. That Frenchman is a man of ill repute and an absolute scoundrel. He swindled my own father out of a small fortune. No doubt he has done to countless others what he has done to you. He belongs in a prison." He paused dramatically. "Or to be dangling from the end of a rope."

"Amen to that," chimed Jonas.

"I am sorry for calling you outlaws," apologized Mr. Denkins. "I meant no disrespect. Clearly, you do not deserve what has been perpetrated against you."

"Think nothing of it, sir. Instead, we should apologize for interrupting your day. My brother and I are grateful for your hospitality and kindness. But truly, we have taken enough of your time. You have a shop to tend." He nodded to Mrs. Denkins. "We thank you for the tea and biscuits. It was delicious. We will see ourselves out."

He and Jonas turned to leave but then Mr. Denkins stopped them. "Wait, Mr. Avery. I think I may be able to help you."

"Whatever do you mean, Husband?" asked his wife, surprised.

He turned to her. "There is that old trunk in the attic ... the one we found tucked away in the hollow place behind the chimney. It was almost as if someone had hidden it there. Don't you remember? It was covered with small boards and an old canvas cloth."

Her eyes lit up with pleasure and surprise. She exclaimed, "Oh, yes! Mr. Magnusson's nephew missed it when he removed all of his uncle's belongings. I once opened the trunk for a look. It has all manner of papers and documents inside. I found nothing interesting or valuable."

"I was going to throw all the papers out and refurbish the trunk," explained Mr. Denkins. "I could probably make use of it in the shop. But I became busy and just never took the time."

"May we see it?" begged Justus. "There may be something inside the trunk that could help lead us to our father."

"Of course," answered Mrs. Denkins. Her eyes twinkled with delight. "And I shall help you with your search!"

Mr. Denkins smiled lovingly at his wife. "I take it, then, that you will not be making any more cups or plates today."

"No, my dear, I am done for the day. No more pottery. These lads need my help."

Her husband grinned. "Well, I reckon one of us needs to try and earn some money. I will go down and reopen the shop." He grabbed a sweet biscuit as he walked by the table and then headed down the stairs. "Give me a shout if you need me for anything."

"I will, dear." Mrs. Denkins turned to the lads and declared, "Now, let's go fetch that old trunk!"

8
THE LETTER

Two Hours Later

Documents and papers were scattered all over the floor of the Denkins' parlor. It was an indescribable mess. Still, despite their thorough search of every document and book contained in the trunk, they had not discovered a single clue as to the whereabouts of Jeremiah Avery.

"Nothing!" moaned Jonas, waving an old ledger in the air. "We've found nothing. We have searched through every single piece of paper. There is nary a word about our father." He held up a leather-bound book. "His indenture was not even mentioned in Magnusson's ledger. How can that be?"

Abigail walked over to the lad and placed a comforting arm around his shoulders. "You musn't give up hope, Jonas. We can check it all again. Perhaps we missed something."

Jonas sighed unhappily. "There is no hope left. We read every word on these papers."

He angrily tossed the useless ledger into the empty trunk. When it impacted against the bottom it made an odd sound. It emitted a dull, hollow thud.

Justus eyed the trunk curiously. "That didn't sound right at all, did it?"

"No, it did not," Mrs. Denkins concurred. "It sounded hollow to me."

Justus stepped toward the trunk. "But this box is made of English oak. It should be solid as rock."

The others joined him. All three of them knelt beside the trunk to investigate. Justus reached inside and rapped on the trunk's bottom with his knuckles. It did, indeed, sound hollow.

"I think this trunk may have a false bottom!" he exclaimed. He turned to Mrs. Denkins. "Do you have a yardstick or some other instrument for measuring?"

"I have a measuring tape," she answered. "I use it for my sewing. Let me fetch it."

She darted toward the door and then scurried down the stairway. She returned seconds later with a ribbon tape that was marked in inches. Justus measured the outside of the trunk. It was exactly twenty-two inches. He then measured the depth inside the trunk. It measured just under twenty inches.

Justus nodded. "There is a two-inch difference."

"What does that mean?" asked Jonas.

"It means there is a gap. It sounds hollow because of the air inside," Justus explained. "There is a thin compartment below the top layer of boards. Accounting for the thickness of the planks, I calculate it to be about one inch in depth. That is not very deep, but something could definitely be hidden there."

The trunk was lined with thick, green felt. If they were going to look for a false bottom, then the lining would have to be torn out.

Justus turned to Abigail. "May I remove the felt lining? I will have to cut it. I'm afraid it will be ruined."

She nodded. "Of course." She clapped her hands together with glee. "Oh, this is so very exciting! To think that I had this great mystery underneath my very own roof. This is like being in a novel or story book."

Justus took his razor-sharp penny knife from his haversack and began cutting. He sliced through the felt that covered the bottom of the trunk. Soon he had the cloth removed. He then examined the boards that had been concealed by the felt. They were all of equal length except for very last board at the rear of the box. It had a small block, roughly six inches in length, in the back left corner. It almost looked like a patch in the wood.

Justus pointed at the inconsistency. "All of the boards are the same except for that one. Do you see how it has been cut?"

"That is strange, indeed," said Jonas. A small remnant of uncut felt remained in the corner, roughly one inch square. It overlapped the small cut block. Jonas tugged at the stray flap of cloth and pulled it loose. When he did it revealed something underneath. There was a design in the wood. It was a fanciful letter "A" stamped into the corner of the board. Beside it was the imprint of a cobbler's hammer.

"Look, Jonas!" Justus exclaimed. "That's Papa's mark!"

"What do you mean, his mark?" inquired Mrs. Denkins, overcome with curiosity. She leaned in closer for a better look.

"Papa had a marking stamp made of steel in his tool kit. When he was done repairing a shoe, he used his hammer to stamp his mark into the leather of the sole. It was his way to identify his handiwork to his customers. Papa was proud of his work as a cobbler." Justus pointed at the image. "That is his mark. I would recognize it anywhere."

She smiled happily. "So, then, your father must have placed the false bottom in this trunk."

Justus nodded. "Indeed. Otherwise, why would he have left his mark? It was his own handiwork. He left it as a sign."

"This must have been your father's trunk," she mused. "Do you remember it?"

Justus thought for a moment. "It could be. I know that when we left home Papa had a trunk with many of our belongings inside it. I just never paid any attention to it. I cannot remember exactly what it looked like."

"Enough of the history lesson," Jonas moaned impatiently. "I'm more worried about that false bottom. Do you reckon Papa hid something in there? Something for us, perhaps?" His eyes twinkled. "Maybe his money?"

Justus shrugged. "There is only one way to find out." He reached down and inserted the blade of his knife into the crack between the boards. He gave a quick flick of his wrist and the piece of wood popped out easily.

"Look!" exclaimed Jonas excitedly. "There *is* something beneath!" Then he frowned. "But it just looks like more papers." He glanced at the mountains of documents scattered about on the floor all around them. "And I don't think we need any more papers."

"These must be different," Justus replied optimistically.

"They have to be important. Otherwise, why would Papa hide them?"

Justus reached into the opening with a trembling hand and retrieved the small bundle of yellowed papers. They were tied together with a piece of string. He tugged at the bow on top of the bundle and untied the string. Quickly, he thumbed through the papers. They were old letters. He instantly recognized his father's handwriting. He also saw some letters that appeared to be in a woman's handwriting. Then he saw his mother's name on one.

"What are they?" asked Jonas. "Did Papa write them?"

Justus nodded. "Some. Mama wrote some of them, too."

"They must be letters exchanged between your parents," marveled Mrs. Denkins. "How romantic! Your father saved them and concealed them inside his trunk."

"Reckon why he kept them hidden in there?" asked Jonas.

Justus shrugged. "They were his most precious possessions, I imagine. Think about it. They were all he had left of Mama. When they threw her overboard, they cast away all of her clothing as well. The crew was terrified of the fever that killed her."

"Your mother was thrown overboard?" exclaimed Mrs. Denkins, aghast. "Why?"

"We told you about our harsh journey to America. Mama was one of many on board ship who died from a fever. All were thrown into the sea in an effort to halt the disease."

"You neglected to tell me that particular part," she moaned. "How barbaric!"

"Such is the way of sea travel," replied Justus. "I am just

glad they did not throw us over, as well. Sometimes entire families went over the rail, sick or no."

She shook her head in utter disbelief. "I simply cannot imagine what you lads have endured. To see your mother cast over the rail of a ship ... it is truly heart-breaking."

"We have our memories of her. More and more, though, I am finding it difficult to remember our mother's face." Jonas smiled. "But I still remember how she smelled, and how it felt to be held by her. I will always remember that."

A tear leaked from Mrs. Denkins' eye, streaking her cheek. "Precious memories, indeed."

Suddenly, Justus gasped. "What's this?" He removed the bottom letter from the stack. "Jonas! This one is addressed to us!"

"What?" his younger brother exclaimed. "How can that be?"

Justus flipped the letter over and examined the wax seal. It bore the same mark as did the trunk, the letter "A" with a tiny cobbler's hammer. "Papa wrote it, for certain. This is his mark."

"But why would he write to us?" asked Jonas. "We were young lads and could not even read and write when last he saw us."

Justus shrugged. "I reckon he had faith that we would learn someday."

"Well, open it, Justus," Mrs. Denkins urged. "We *must* see the message he left for you!"

Quickly, Justus cracked the hard wax seal and unfolded the letter. It was very long and included two sheets of paper. He smiled when he saw the introduction. He read silently for a moment and then, suddenly, Jonas punched him in the shoulder.

"Read it out loud!" the younger lad demanded.

"Sorry," Justus apologized. He turned to Mrs. Denkins. "Would you mind reading it to us?"

She knit her brow. "I thought you said you can read."

"I can ... we both can. But I saw a few unfamiliar words. And mostly what we have read before has been in books or newspapers. I am not experienced in reading handwritten notes or correspondences. I think it would be better if you read it to both of us. We would be most grateful."

She smiled as she took the letter in hand. "It will be my honor and pleasure." She pointed to a date at the top of the page. "It is dated May 1, 1773."

"That was almost two years ago," said Jonas. "It has been hidden away for a long time."

"That was shortly before we bought the building from Mr. Magnusson's nephew," remarked Mrs. Denkins. "Perhaps that is why your father wrote the letter and concealed it in the trunk. He was about to go and wanted to leave a message for you."

"Then he hid the trunk and its contents out of sight up in your attic," added Justus.

She nodded. "And, hopefully, this letter will tell us where he went. Let's find out."

She cleared her throat and read:

My Dearest Sons,

I want you to know that you are both dear to my heart and that I desire desperately to find you. I write this letter today with the hope that it will someday find its way into your hands.

I know that you are both clever lads. I have faith that you will one day discover the trunk and the hidden compartment where I concealed it for you. I pray that, once discovered, this letter will help you to find your way back to me. It now seems this is my only hope for the reunion of our family.

I do not know if you will recall the events that led to our separation. You were both so very young when tragedy divided us. I was severely injured in a fall from the ship's rigging near the end of our journey to America. My legs were broken, and I suffered a terrible blow to the head. Crewmen took me to a local hospital where, in time, my body recovered. However, for a long time my mind did not. The injury to my head all but erased my memory. When I awoke, I could not remember any details of my life before waking inside that hospital. Needless to say, it was a very frightening circumstance for me. My only clues to my identity were my name, my trunk of personal belongings, and a box of very old and well-used cobbler's tools.

I was in the hospital for many weeks. In time I became well enough to leave. However, I owed a large debt to the surgeon that I could not repay. He eventually sold me into indentured servitude as payment for my debt. Edward Magnusson of Baltimore City purchased my indenture because of my potential skills as a cobbler. I am so very glad that he did. He was a good man and very kind to me.

Unfortunately, my loss of memory continued to afflict me for some time. It took several months, but my memories eventually began to return, as well as my skills in cobbling. The items contained inside my trunk helped me to remember many things, as well. The letters that I exchanged with your dear mother many years ago were most helpful of all. I have attached them to this note. I pray that you will cherish them and keep them, and they will also help you to remember her, God rest her soul.

Once my memory and strength returned in full, I began to search for you in earnest. Mr. Magnusson assisted me. We have looked for you for over two years, but our efforts have been in vain. I have been unable to locate Captain Rochelle. It seems that he no longer docks his ship in Baltimore. I have, however, spoken to several men who have made known to me his dubious and criminal character. I have been told that many times in the past he has separated children from their families and then sold them into servitude. I fear this happened to you. I pray that it has not.

Still, I shall never give up on you. You are my sons. For as long as I live, I shall look for you whenever and wherever I can. However, my future efforts will no longer be centered in Baltimore. Mr. Magnusson's heir has sold my indenture to a fellow named Arthur Treadway in the village of Upper Marlborough, Maryland. Once I am established there, I will continue my search for you. If you ever find this letter, then you must go there and seek me. I will be waiting for you.

Please know that I love you and miss you very much. My memories of you fill my heart to overflowing. They give me the strength and will to face each new day. I pray that, someday, we may once again make new memories together.

Your faithful and loving father,

Jeremiah Avery

There was a long moment of silence as they contemplated the touching, emotional words recorded in the letter. All of them had tears streaking their cheeks.

Finally, Jonas declared, "That was a good letter. Papa remembers us." He wiped the tears from his cheeks.

"And he has been looking for us," added Justus, smiling.

Jonas nodded. "We must go now to where he is and find him."

"It should be easy enough. The letter says he was headed to Upper Marlborough. We know where that is."

"Huh?" asked Jonas, confused.

"Upper Marlborough," repeated Justus. "Don't you remember? The *Sleeping Bear Tavern*? Our friend, Charity?"

Jonas' eyes widened in realization. He slapped his hand against his forehead. "Of course! Upper Marlborough!" He marveled, "And to think that we were just there only a few days ago. We may even have passed Papa on the street."

Justus nodded. "Could be." He chuckled. "Wouldn't that be something?"

Mrs. Denkins interrupted their jubilation. "Lads, there is something else here. It is most odd. I almost missed it. It was concealed beneath a narrow fold along the edge of the paper."

"What is it?" asked Justus, instantly curious.

"There is a brief poem jotted there. The script is very small."

"A poem?" queried Jonas, confused. "Why would Papa write a poem?"

She shook her head. "I do not know. Was your father a poet?"

Justus laughed. "Not likely."

"Well, he has written one at the end of this letter. I do not understand what it means. It is a mystery to me."

"Read it," begged Jonas, glancing over her shoulder.

"Very well. See if you can make any sense of this."

"Once in hand, ye sons of man, trusty tool of timber and steel;
Weigh carefully, lads, lest ye strike, a secret to reveal."

"What kind of poem is that?" asked Jonas, scratching his head.

"It is not a poem at all," answered his brother. "It is a riddle." He cut a sideways glance at his brother. "And I think it is a clue."

"A clue to what?"

"A clue to his location, perhaps?" postulated Mrs. Denkins.

Justus shook his head. "He has already told us where he is going. We have the name of the town and his new master. That is more than enough information to find him."

"Then it *must* be about his money," declared Jonas.

"But that makes no sense at all," said Mrs. Denkins. "He said in his letter that his memory has returned. If his memory is complete, and includes the memory of his personal fortune, then why has he remained captive and in servitude? Why not simply use some of the money and pay off his debt? He could be a free man and then go about his business."

"Because paying his debt of servitude might consume a large portion of his savings," declared Justus. "Then he would not have enough money to purchase land. A farm of his own has always been his dream. Indeed, it was his dream for all of us."

"So, then, you think your father remains an indentured servant in order to provide a home and future for you?" marveled Mrs. Denkins.

Justus nodded. "I believe so."

"What a good and noble man your father must be. He is sacrificing his own freedom for the benefit of his sons."

She smiled admiringly. "I hope that I shall meet him someday."

"So, what is this poem all about?" interrupted Jonas impatiently. "Is he trying to tell us where to find his treasure or not?"

Justus growled under his breath. "I have told you before, Jonas. I do not like that word. Papa had no treasure. He only had the money that he saved over a lifetime of work. He intended to purchase a farm with it." He shook his head. "It just makes me so angry. All these people are hunting for him like he is some kind of criminal or pirate! Papa has no chest full of silver and gold. At most he possessed a few gold and silver coins."

"Even a tiny purse of gold and silver coins is a treasure here in America," explained Mrs. Denkins. "Most folk here have never even seen a gold coin, much less a handful of them. If your father does, indeed, possess a life savings in silver and gold, then to most folk it would, indeed, seem like a treasure."

"And worth hunting him for," added Justus. "But why are Captain Rochelle and our former master searching so diligently for him? Surely, they already have plenty of money."

Mrs. Denkins explained, "Men who have an abundance of money are all the more afflicted with the sickness of greed. They will always strive for more ... even for your father's tiny fortune. You musn't let them have it!" She placed the letter in Justus' hand. "That is why you boys must find him first. You have another clue. Now what will you do?"

Justus cut a steely glance at his younger brother. "We

will depart immediately for Upper Marlborough. We must find Papa before they do!"

9
ESCAPE!

At long last Justus and Jonas were getting out of Baltimore. They headed west, toward the junction with the highway that would lead them southward toward Upper Marlborough. The sun was setting rapidly. The streets of the city were filled with folk tired from a long day's work. The numerous taverns and restaurants were filled with hungry patrons in search of supper. Soon, however, Baltimore would grow quiet as its citizens returned to their homes and hearths.

"Should we just wait and leave in the morning?" asked Jonas, yawning. "There must be a room available in one of these taverns. I'm tired."

Justus shook his head. "No, we need to go now. We are running short of money. Besides, I do not wish to remain in this city any longer. Our work here is done. We found what we came here for. We know where Papa has gone. It is time for us to go."

"Shouldn't we at least have supper before we go too

far? We have not eaten since breakfast. And you know how ill-tempered I get when I'm hungry."

Justus grinned at his younger brother. "I reckon we can eat." He pointed to a nearby tavern. "How about that place?"

Jonas eyed the tavern hungrily. The sign over the door identified the establishment as *The Bristly Boar.* "That'll do," he declared. "With a sign like that one they must have pork on the plate. I wouldn't mind a bit of smoked hog."

The boys crossed the street to the tavern and then entered. It was dark, smoky, and crowded inside. They found a small, unoccupied table in the back corner of the room. Soon one of the tavern girls brought their meal. They enjoyed hickory-smoked pork, boiled potatoes, baked apples, fresh bread, and tart apple cider. The food was hot and tasty, and there was plenty of it. They ate until they were satisfied. Once filled, Jonas burped and then leaned back lazily in his chair. His eyes were heavy with fatigue.

"Don't get too comfortable," Justus warned, kicking the leg of his brother's chair to rouse him. "We have a long night of travel ahead of us. I'll not carry you to where we're going."

Jonas sat up straight and then took a drink of cold cider. "Very well, then. What is our plan for the journey?"

"We start walking. That is the plan. As best I recall, Upper Marlborough is about twenty-five miles to the south. We should be able to walk it in a couple of days."

"How far will we go tonight?" asked Jonas.

"Not far. We just need to get clear of Baltimore City. We can make camp in the woods somewhere along the highway. The weather is pleasant enough for camping.

Then, after a good night's sleep, we will get back on the road. I plan to hike most of those miles tomorrow."

"It will be good to be out in the woods again," acknowledged Jonas with a sigh. "I have not slept well since we arrived in this city. It is just too busy and loud."

Justus nodded. "It certainly is." He took a final swig of his cider. "Are you ready to go?"

"I need to visit the outhouse first," confessed Jonas, standing. "Do not leave me."

Justus chuckled. "I won't. Go take care of your personal business and I will pay the bill."

"Be sure to get us some extra meat and bread for tomorrow's breakfast."

"Good idea," said Justus. "Do not tarry. We need to get moving."

"I won't be long." Jonas pushed his chair into place beneath the table and then quickly headed for the door.

Justus waved to the tavern girl. When she came to his table, he ordered food for their journey. She returned minutes later with a linen-wrapped bundle. Justus paid the bill. Several minutes passed. Jonas had been gone for an unusually long time. Justus was beginning to wonder what was keeping him. Soon, however, Jonas came bursting through the tavern door. He almost sprinted across the crowded room. His face was red and filled with worry. He carried a folded piece of paper in his hand.

"What is wrong with you?" demanded Justus as soon as his brother came within earshot.

"This!" responded Jonas, tossing the paper onto the table.

Justus picked it up. It was a poster advertising a reward for their capture. It was almost identical to the one that

Charity had shown them the previous week when they were in Upper Marlborough. The only difference was the size of the reward. It had been doubled. Their bounty now stood at twenty British pounds paid in silver.

"Where did you get this?" Justus asked, instantly concerned.

"It was nailed to the door of the outhouse!" He pulled back his chair and then sat down. "After I found this one, I took a quick stroll along the street. Those cursed things are hanging on every post and storefront!"

Justus grimaced. "Sledge is still hunting for us." He shook his head. "This large reward will be difficult to ignore. It is equal to a year's wages for a common man. And here we sit in a public house. We should have been more careful." He met his brother's gaze. "Do you think anyone has recognized us?"

Jonas shrugged. "I don't know. But I would rather not wait around and find out."

Both boys scanned the room. No one appeared to be paying attention to them. Then, suddenly, Justus noticed two men at a distant table. The men were staring in their direction. One of them leaned in close to the other and whispered something. The other fellow nodded, then he reached inside his pocket and took out a piece of paper. Together they studied the paper. Then, without uttering another word, one of the men stood and walked toward the door. He departed the tavern with haste.

"I do not like the looks of this," hissed Justus. "I think the fellow who just left has spotted us. He may be going to report us to the sheriff."

"Or to Sledge." Jonas leaned in close. "What should we do?"

"We need to slip out of here and get moving. The more miles we can put between us and this city the better. Now I think we should just forget about camping tonight. We must walk through the night. We can rest after sunrise."

Jonas nodded. "I agree. There is no time to waste. Let's go!"

The two brothers moved swiftly toward the door. Jonas got there first. He lifted the latch and then opened the door just as another fellow was pushing it open to enter the tavern. The man stumbled slightly, and they bumped into one another.

"Pardon me, sir," begged Jonas politely.

Suddenly, Jonas gasped. He recognized the man with whom he had collided. He was standing face-to-face with John Bailey! And right behind Bailey was Abram Sledge and the man who had moments ago been staring at them from across the room.

"He was right! It *is* you!" shouted Sledge in disbelief.

"That's them, ain't it?" exclaimed the tattletale. "I told you, Mr. Sledge! I told you! It's them runaway boys! I want my reward right now!"

Jonas, without even thinking, reared back his foot and delivered a vicious kick to John Bailey's shin. The man doubled over and grasped his leg, howling loudly from the pain. Justus lunged past his brother and bull-rushed Abram Sledge, knocking him into the other fellow who was with them. Both men tumbled backwards and landed in the street with resounding thuds. A cloud of street dust hovered around them.

"Come on, Jonas!" Justus shouted frantically.

The boys wasted no time. They sprinted down the street, desperate to escape their pursuers.

"I'll get them, Mr. Sledge!" screeched John Bailey as he limped out of the tavern.

He whipped a pistol from his belt and aimed at the fleeing boys. Sledge shouted and slapped Bailey's arm just as he pulled the trigger. The flintlock discharged harmlessly into the dirt road near his feet.

"What are you doing?" scolded Sledge angrily. "Those lads are no good to us dead! Put that gun away!"

"I ... I'm sorry, Mr. Sledge," pleaded Bailey. "I reckon I wasn't thinking straight."

"No. You were not thinking at all." Sledge scowled. "From now on, you do not act unless I tell you to."

Bailey appeared much afraid. "Yes, sir. I am sorry, sir."

"As well you should be." He turned and watched the boys running away. He smiled deviously. "Worry not. They cannot go far. We shall have them in hand soon enough." He turned to John Bailey. "Pay the man his reward and then go fetch our horses and hounds. I plan to have these lads in chains before the sunrise."

THE BOYS HAD COVERED ALMOST A HUNDRED YARDS when the sharp crack of a pistol echoed through the night. Both lads ducked instinctively.

"They're shooting at us!" wailed Jonas. "Sledge means to kill us!"

"Run faster!" his brother urged. He pointed to their left. There was an open alley between two storefronts. "There! The alleyway! Let's take cover between the buildings!"

Quick as a flash, the two boys darted into the mouth of

the dark alley. As he turned the corner, Justus slowed down and stole a quick glance back down the street. It did not appear that anyone was following them. There was, however, an excited gaggle of men gathered in front of the tavern. Justus could not be certain, but it appeared that Abram Sledge was scolding John Bailey.

"Don't stop now!" begged Jonas. "They are coming for us with guns!"

Justus nodded. Onward they ran. If Sledge somehow managed to catch them their entire mission would be foiled. Indeed, they would be returned to servitude and never find their father. They simply could not allow themselves to be captured. For now, escaping Sledge and fleeing Baltimore were their only priorities.

Soon they emerged onto a service road that ran along the back of the stores. They paused for a moment to get their bearings and make a plan.

"We must go this way," urged Jonas, pointing to his right. "That will take us further away from Sledge."

Justus looked back and forth in both directions. He considered for a moment and then shook his head. "No, we should go left and double back on them. They will never expect it."

"You want us to go back in their direction?" groaned Jonas in disbelief.

"I tell you, Jonas, they will never anticipate such a move. They will assume that we have continued on toward the east and are attempting to put more distance between us. But if we just keep running a straight line in that direction then we are bound to get caught."

"So, then, where do we go?" challenged Jonas impatiently.

Justus pointed left. "If we go back to the west and then find another alley that leads to the north, then we can make our escape. We can do the same on the next block and then the block after that. We can put several city blocks and lots of buildings between ourselves and Sledge if we just use our wits."

Jonas chuckled and nodded. "Outwitting Sledge should not be all that hard. We've done a good job so far." Somewhere in the distance there came the lonely crooning of bloodhounds. Jonas' eyes grew wide with fear. He moaned, "Oh, no. Sledge has loosed his hounds."

"It does not matter. He is just trying to frighten us."

"Well, it's working," responded Jonas. "I remember well those hounds chasing us through the woods. They almost caught us, remember?"

"Yes, but that was in the open forest. Those dogs will never be able to smell us amongst all the other people and animals that have filled these city streets today. They may actually be a blessing in disguise. If the dogs get confused by all the scents, it could actually buy us a little more time." Justus gave his little brother a firm slap on the shoulder. "Are you ready to run?"

Jonas nodded. "I'm ready to get out of this city and far away from Sledge."

"Good. Then let's not waste another minute. Come on!"

They sprinted west along the service road. From somewhere beyond the building on their left the mournful baying of the bloodhounds grew louder.

THE HOUR WAS GROWING LATE. DARKNESS AND SILENCE shrouded the city. The brothers had been on the run for almost an hour. They traveled a twisted, random route, weaving their way through a labyrinth of buildings, empty lots, alleys, and side streets. They stopped on occasion to rest and listen. It had been quite some time since they had heard the shouting of men or the barking of hounds. It appeared that they had once again escaped Sledge.

As they were making their way along a quiet side street, Justus pointed to a narrow, tunnel-like alley that led between two brick buildings. "Let's hide in there and figure out what we are going to do next."

Jonas nodded and instantly followed his brother into the dark alley. They concealed themselves between two large wooden barrels that were resting against one of the walls. They waited, silent, and listened for any movement along the street. There was none.

"I'm pretty sure we lost them," declared Jonas.

"It appears so," concurred his brother.

Jonas peered toward the back of the long alley. "Where are we, exactly?"

Justus sighed. "I am not certain. I know we were moving in a general westerly direction, but then I think we took a turn toward the south. Still, with no sun in the sky, I cannot be sure."

Suddenly, they heard a door open near the back of the alley, a mere twenty feet away. The yellow light of candles and lanterns invaded the darkness, casting a dull glow upon the brick walls of the tall buildings. The boys flattened themselves against the wall in an effort to remain in the shadows cast by the barrels. Then voices broke the silence of the night. Two men were conversing.

"Do you have everything, Andrew?" asked one of the men.

"I have loaded all of the goods on your manifest, Mr. Oliver," answered the fellow named Andrew. "There are forty bolts of linens, wools, and broadcloth and four cases of yarn and thread. It is a full load, to be sure."

"Did you cover my cloth well?" inquired the other man. "I have a lot of money invested in that load. My partners in Alexandria have paid well and expect a high-quality and undamaged product. My reputation as a weaver will be ruined if those cloths get wet."

"Do not worry, Mr. Oliver. The skies are clear this night. Besides, I have covered your goods with two waterproof oilcloths and tied them down well. Your cloth is in good hands. My wagon company is the best in the business, and I am their most trusted driver."

"How long before you go?"

"I am going to fetch myself a hot meal and then I will get on the road. I plan to ride through the night. I will meet up with my relief driver in Upper Marlborough at first light."

"That is nigh-on thirty miles," said Mr. Oliver. "Are you sure you can make such a long distance in one night?"

"I do it twice every week, sir. I know every dip and rut in that highway. I shall be there before breakfast."

"Excellent," responded the weaver named Mr. Oliver. "I wish you safe travels, Andrew. Good night."

"Good night to you, Mr. Oliver."

All light disappeared when the shop owner closed the rear door to his shop. Once again darkness descended upon the alleyway. Justus and Jonas listened to the crunching of rock and gravel as the wagon driver walked away from them. He was moving toward the back of the alley. Soon the sound of his footsteps faded into the night.

"Did you hear that?" whispered Justus, elated. "The driver is headed to Upper Marlborough!"

Jonas grinned and nodded. "Are you thinking what I am thinking?"

"Yes ... if you are thinking we should stow away in that wagon and get a free ride."

"That is *exactly* what I am thinking," answered Jonas.

"Then let's go. We must get inside and under cover before the driver returns."

The boys peeked from behind the barrels and then, seeing no one, crept toward the back of the alley. Once around the corner they spotted a wagon that was covered with oil cloths. The two-horse team that would pull the wagon was tied to a hitching post.

"Move quickly and quietly," urged Justus in a low whisper.

The boys scurried to the rear of the wagon, lifted the oilcloth, and then silently climbed into the wagon bed. They crawled over and between rolls of linen and wool cloth. They soon found an open gap in the load near the center of the wagon. It was tight but reasonably comfortable, and a perfect hiding place. They settled into the space and waited, breathless.

"Do you think the driver will suspect anything?" whispered Jonas.

His brother reached over and gave him a reassuring squeeze on his shoulder. He answered quietly, "He will never know we are here. We are perfectly safe."

A few minutes later they heard footsteps and a man whistling. The man spoke kindly to his horses. Seconds later they felt the wagon shudder as the man climbed onto his seat. And then, suddenly, they were moving. The wagon swayed gently as is plodded along the rutted roadway. Soon the exhausted boys gave in to the rhythmic motion of the wagon. They fell fast asleep.

JUSTUS AWAKENED WITH A START. THE WAGON WAS NO longer moving. He was thoroughly disoriented and for a moment forgot where he lay. Then he heard the wagon driver speak to someone. Instantly the memories of the previous night came flooding into his mind. He remembered their frantic flight from Sledge and then stowing away inside the cargo wagon.

He reached over and gave his brother a shake. Jonas' eyes fluttered open. The younger lad began to speak but then Justus lifted a finger of caution to his lips. Jonas nodded. They listened and remained completely silent. The wagon driver's voice soon faded into the distance. Somewhere they heard a door open and then close.

Jonas leaned in close to Justus' ear. He whispered, "Where did he go?"

Justus shrugged. "I do not know. To breakfast, perhaps?" he pointed to a tiny stream of light that was glowing through a hole in the oilcloth. "The sun is up, or soon will be."

"But where are we?" asked Jonas. "Have we reached Upper Marlborough?"

Justus pointed to a larger hole in the cloth near the side of the wagon. "I will steal a look."

He crawled silently over two large bolts of cloth and

then moved his eye close to the hole. His heart leapt with joy when he saw a familiar sign hanging on the front of a nearby building. It was an image of a slumbering black bear. The sign read, *Sleeping Bear Tavern*. They were, indeed, in Upper Marlborough! Justus quickly crawled back to his brother, a smile filling his face.

"Are we there?" whispered Jonas.

"We are. And we are parked right in front of the *Sleeping Bear*."

Jonas sighed happily. "We made it! I can scarcely believe it."

"Indeed. Now let's get moving."

Minutes later the boys slipped over the tailgate of the wagon. It was early morning. The street was abandoned. Though the eastern sky shone with a purple-orange glow, the sun was not quite above the treetops. They quickly made their way down the empty street toward the edge of town. Soon they crossed a stone bridge over a small creek.

"We are leaving town?" Jonas asked. "Where are we going?"

"To Charity's house. Don't you remember?" He pointed to a narrow path to their right that led into the forest. "It is down yonder in the woods. We will hide there for a while. Once we can be sure no one has seen or recognized us, we will get a message to her."

Jonas grinned and licked his lips. "I sure hope she can bring us some breakfast. I'm near starved."

10
LYING LOW

Mid-Morning

"What do you think?" asked Justus, handing the letter to his brother.

Jonas scanned the note that Justus had written for their friend, Charity. It read:

Dear Miss MacLellan,

We have returned from Baltimore City with news of our father. We humbly request your assistance. We are hiding out in a place that you know well. Please come soon and bring food. We eagerly and hungrily await your presence.

J. A.

"Short and to the point," remarked Jonas. "I like it. How do you plan to get it to her?"

"There is a young lad who works at the livery stable at the edge of town, just beyond the bridge. I noticed him when we passed there last week. I will attempt to hire him to deliver it."

"But can you trust him? We do not know this lad."

Justus grinned and held up two copper coins. "These should buy his service and his silence." He stood and then strode toward the door. "You stay here. I will go and get it done."

"Be careful. Don't get caught."

Justus lifted the latch, paused, and smiled confidently at his brother. "I don't intend to."

❦

JUSTUS ENTERED THE OUTSKIRTS OF TOWN WITHOUT incident. He hid in a thicket of pines near the livery stable and waited for the boy who worked there to make an appearance. He did not have to wait long. Less than five minutes later the young fellow came out of the stable leading a horse toward a nearby pen. He appeared to be around Jonas' age. The lad opened the gate, placed the horse inside the pen, and then closed and latched the gate. He was walking back toward the stable when he heard a low whistle. He paused, curious, and listened.

Justus stepped out of the shadow of the trees and waved. He motioned to the boy to come to him and then stepped back into the concealment of the thicket. The boy glanced left and right, his eyes filled with suspicion. Nevertheless, he appeared intrigued. Once more Justus stepped into the sunlight and motioned to him. He smiled a disarming smile, held up a coin so that it glistened in the sunlight, and then once again retreated into the shadows of the trees. The boy hesitated for a moment and then slowly meandered toward the spot where he had last seen Justus. Seconds later he entered the thick grove of pines.

"Thank you for coming," declared Justus, stepping from behind the trunk of a large tree.

"Why you be out here hidin' in the woods?" asked the boy in a heavy Scottish accent. His tone betrayed his obvious suspicion.

"I have my reasons," Justus answered. "My name is Justus. What is yours?"

"Craig MacLellan."

"Does your father own the stable?"

The lad chuckled. "Not likely, seeing as how he lays in yon cemetery beyond the creek alongside my ma, God rest her soul. No, I am no son of a stablemaster. Rather, I am his humble servant, indentured for the next seven years."

"You are a MacLellan?" Justus confirmed. "Do you know Charity MacLellan?"

"Aye. She is a cousin of mine. Just this very mornin' I saw her down at the *Sleeping Bear*. She fed me a fine breakfast."

"Might I hire you to deliver a message to her?"

The lad smiled mischievously. "That depends on how much you are a payin'."

Justus held up two copper half-pennies. "Will this do?"

"Aye. That'll do just fine." He reached for the coins. He examined them quickly, nodded, and then stuffed them into the pocket of his dirty, threadbare coat.

Justus gave the lad his letter. "It is important that you get this to her as quickly as possible. Do you understand?"

The boy nodded. He hesitated and then gave Justus a thorough and thoughtful looking-over. "Wait ... I recognize you! You're one of those lads on the wanted posters. A runaway from Virginia, you are. Charity told me all about you. Avery is your name."

Justus frowned. "Does that mean you are going to turn me in to the sheriff?"

The lad's lip curled into a friendly grin. "Nah. Your secret is safe with me, Mr. Avery. I'm actually half a mind to be a runnin' off with you. Lord knows anything would be better than remainin' here with my no-good master." He tipped his hat to Justus. "I'll get this note to Charity straightaway. 'Twill be dinner time soon. I was a plannin' to go and beg for me a scrap of bread from the *Sleeping Bear*. Thanks to you, though, I can buy me a whole loaf." He grinned happily.

"Thank you, Craig. Sincerely."

"You are most welcome. 'Tis no trouble a'tall."

He turned and departed the thicket. Justus retreated into the woods in the direction of the hideout.

Mid-Afternoon

JUSTUS AND JONAS WERE NAPPING ATOP A MAKESHIFT pine needle mattress when the latch lifted on the door. Charity Maclellan entered, smiling broadly, and carrying a basket covered with white linen. Justus and Jonas sat up, both surprised and somewhat groggy from sleep. Charity placed her basket on the table and then faced the boys, her hands resting on her hips. She shot them a glare of pretend displeasure.

"What a fine pair of outlaws you are ... sleeping the day away! 'Tis is a good thing I am not the sheriff. You two ruffians would be shackled and in the jailhouse for sure."

Justus grinned sheepishly. "We knew it was you. Who else would be wandering out here into these woods?" He stood up and walked to her. "It is good to see you again, Charity."

Charity offered her hand. Justus took it like a gentleman and then kissed her knuckles.

"It is good to be seen," she answered, her face flushing red. She beamed with pleasure.

Jonas appeared at his brother's side. "I hope those are hot vittles in your basket!" He licked his lips hungrily.

"I brought you some smoked turkey, potato fritters, buttery peas, and apple tarts. They were amongst the left-overs from today's dinner."

"I will, of course, pay you for the meal," insisted Justus.

She smiled. "And I will accept." She motioned to the table. "Now sit whilst I prepare your plates. But first, did you find out anything about your father?"

Jonas nodded eagerly. "We sure did! We found an important clue that brought us straight back here to Upper Marlborough!"

Charity's eyes widened with surprise. "Is that so?" Once again, she pointed to the table. "Your dinner is getting cold. Sit and eat. Then you must tell me *everything*, and quickly so. I must return to the tavern before it is time for supper service."

One Hour Later

CHARITY EMITTED A LOW WHISTLE AND SHOOK HER head in disbelief. "So then, the man with the dogs truly took a shot at you?"

Jonas nodded. "He or the other fellow, John Bailey. I have never been so frightened in all my life." He placed his now-empty plate atop Charity's basket.

"Let me get this all straight in my mind. You found the *Almshouse Hospital*, but it was closed. You broke into another hospital to steal the records from the *Almshouse Hospital*. You discovered your father was indentured and then found the place where he once lived and worked. But the cobbler's shop is now a pottery shop. Then you found a clue hidden inside your father's old trunk, got shot at and chased by hounds, and then escaped Baltimore by hiding away in the bed of a cargo wagon."

"That about sums it up," confessed Justus, grinning. "But it all sounds much more adventurous that it really was, I think."

Charity shook her head in disbelief. "No, I believe that it was all quite adventurous ... and dangerous. You lads have been busy."

Justus nodded. "Very. It took some doing, but we now know the name of the man who bought our father's indenture from the heir of his first master. And, what's more, we know that he lives here in this township."

"Right here ... in Upper Marlborough?" she asked in disbelief. "What a coincidence!"

"Indeed," responded Justus. "If we had only known beforehand then we might have avoided the dangers and frustrations of Baltimore City altogether." He sighed and shook his head. "We were lucky to get out of there in one piece."

"What is this fellow's name ... the one who now owns your father's indenture? Surely, I have heard of him," declared Charity.

Justus fished the letter from his father from the pocket of his waistcoat. He scanned down the page until he saw the name. "Ah ... here it is. Arthur Treadway."

She smiled. "Now there is a familiar name! I knew Mr. Treadway. He was a delightful old fellow. He owned a sizeable plantation east of town."

"Knew?" echoed Jonas, narrowing his gaze. His voice cracked with emotion. "Was?"

She frowned and nodded. "He died about a year ago."

Silence descended upon the room. Jonas turned to his brother, staring at him through mournful eyes. "I *knew* it was too good to be true! It is just another dead end!"

"It is *not* a dead end," Justus reassured him. "The plantation is still there, along with all the slaves and servants. It simply has a new owner." He glanced at Charity. "Correct?"

Charity nodded. "Yes, indeed. Mr. Treadway's oldest son, Albert, inherited the place."

"But why would Mr. Treadway indenture a cobbler in the first place?" asked Jonas. "Did he own a shoe shop?"

Charity shook her head. "No. He was a tobacco farmer. But you must understand the size of his plantation. It was probably over 3,000 acres. He owned at least a hundred slaves and indentured as many more. Keeping his workers in shoes was likely a full-time job."

Justus nodded. "That makes sense. And Papa did not only work on shoes. He could do all sorts of leather work. I am sure that his skills would be put to use in other ways."

"No doubt he would be most valuable on a large plantation," affirmed Charity. "In addition to shoes, he could repair saddles, tools, and such. I imagine he is still there."

"The riddle!" exclaimed Jonas. "Show her the riddle!"

"What riddle?" inquired Charity, instantly intrigued.

"There was a mysterious verse in the letter that Papa left us. It is quite a mystery," explained Justus as he retrieved the letter from his pocket.

He unfolded the letter and then read the perplexing riddle:

"Once in hand, ye sons of man, trusty tool of timber and steel;
Weigh carefully, lads, lest ye strike, a secret to reveal."

"How utterly odd," marveled Charity. She glanced at Justus. "What does it mean?"

He shook his head. "We have absolutely no idea. But it must contain a secret message for us, or else why would Papa include it in the margins our letter?"

She nodded. "I quite agree. You absolutely *must* solve this riddle. Surely it is the key to everything you seek."

"We have tried," declared Jonas. "But, so far, we've not been able to figure it out."

"You musn't give up." Charity glanced out the window and then stood. "Gentlemen, time has gotten away from me. I have greatly enjoyed the account of all your adventures. And this mysterious riddle makes everything all the more intriguing. But now the hour is growing late. I must return to the real world and get back to the tavern and do my work."

Justus and Jonas stood and escorted her to the door.

"Thank you for the meal," declared Justus. "It was much needed and very delicious."

"And for this house," added Jonas. "You are very kind to allow us to hide here."

"You are most welcome, of course." She paused beside the open door. "I know a few of the servants from the Treadway estate. One of them is a driver. He comes to town a couple of times each week for supplies. It may take a day or two, but when I see him, I will inquire about your father. Meanwhile, you must remain here and keep out of sight. Don't go near the town."

"What of food and supplies?" asked Justus.

"I will send my cousin, Craig, a couple of times a day with food and necessities. I will return to see you myself once I have news of your father."

Justus nodded. "We cannot thank you enough." He reached into his pocket and fished out a handful of copper and silver coins. It was all that he had left of the money that Drusilla Dawson had given them. He offered the coins the palm of his hand. "Take whatever you need to cover our expenses."

Charity took five copper pennies. "That should suffice for at least the next three days."

"That does not seem like much. I have a little more if you need it," Justus assured her. "But our funds are running low. We burned through them pretty quickly in Baltimore City."

"It will do for now. My master sells me the daily left-overs for a bargain price." She smiled. "And I would not let you starve, money or no." She nodded politely. "Good day to you both."

"And to you," answered Justus, smiling.

"Goodbye, Charity," chirped Jonas.

She opened the door and departed quickly. Jonas closed it behind her and then turned to his brother.

"What now?" he asked.

"We lay low, eat, sleep, and wait," answered his big brother.

Jonas grinned happily. "I can do that."

The Next Evening

"It's almost dark," announced Jonas, lounging lazily on his bed of blanket-covered pine needles. "Surely Craig will be along soon. Breakfast is but a memory now. I'm ready to eat."

"He promised he would come at sundown," Justus reassured him.

"He said the cooks were preparing chicken pies for supper tonight." Jonas licked his lips. "I love chicken pie."

Justus ignored his brother's hungry ramblings. He was seated near the hearth and staring in the firelight at the letter from his father. He focused his attention on the perplexing words of the strange riddle. The more he studied it the more frustrated he became. Try as he might he could make no sense of the mysterious little poem. A soft knock at the door interrupted his thoughts.

"It's Craig!" exclaimed Jonas. "Supper is here!" He rolled off of his pine needle bed and darted toward the door.

Justus stood, placed the letter on the mantle, and then went to greet their young friend. Jonas opened the latch and let the boy in. Craig MacLellan entered, basket in hand and a warm smile filling his dirt-streaked, freckled face.

He announced, "Charity has outdone herself tonight, fellows. She sent three chicken pies, three loaves of fresh bread, and three ears of roasted corn." He reached into his pocket and produced a small tin box. "And she sent a tin full of tea so that you can fix yourself a brew."

"What about a teapot?" asked Jonas. "We have none here."

"It is in the basket," the boy explained as he placed his cargo on the eating table. "And Charity told me to wish you all a happy supper."

"Why three of everything?" teased Justus, a knowing smile filling his face.

The young lad raised an eyebrow. "Because you shall be havin' company for supper this evenin'." He reached into the basket and then produced three plates and three spoons. "Let's eat before these pies get cold!"

"This will be the second time this day you've taken a meal with us, Craig. Am I paying for all your food now?" teased Justus.

"'Tis merely the cost of delivery." He winked. "And my silence. It is quite a bargain, really. Either you feed me, or I shall be forced to fetch the sheriff."

Justus chuckled. "We are at your mercy, I suppose."

Craig nodded. "Yes. Yes, you are. Now, enough of this idle talk. There be eatin' to do!"

The three young fellows sat down at the table and attacked the delicious food with gusto. A half-hour later the boys were well-fed and satisfied. They sat together, cross-legged, in front of the hearth. They sipped hot, sweet tea and shared stories and tales.

There was much laughter. It was a good thing to have a new friend. Justus and Jonas were truly happy and content. It had been a long time since they had been so.

Justus nodded toward the window. "The hour is late. Won't your master be missing you soon?"

Craig shook his head. "He cares not where I go at night, so long as I am in the stables at sunup and working all the long day. I come and go as I please when the sun goes down."

Justus nodded. "Does he take good care of you?"

Craig chuckled. "He doesn't take care of me a'tall. He feeds me a little from time to time, mostly parched corn or rice, but that is about it."

"What about a home? Where do you stay?" asked Jonas.

"I sleep in the stable loft," answered Craig, taking another sip of his tea.

"What's it like to live in a stable loft?" asked Justus.

"Scorching hot in the summer and freezing cold in the winter, just as one might expect." He grinned. "Actually, it is not all bad. My master leaves me alone most of the time, so long as I work and show him respect. He rarely beats me. I cannot complain." He paused. "And Charity has been a big help to me over the years. She is a fine young woman, and she is my only family."

Justus asked hesitatingly, "When did you lose your folks?"

"Four years ago ... I was but eight years old. They died of the same fever that took Charity's mother. Since there was no one in my family who could take me in, the county declared me an orphan and then Mr. Tolbert, the liveryman, bought my indenture." He frowned. "They sold me at the courthouse like I was a farm mule."

Justus patted his new friend on the shoulder. "We know well how that feels."

"Aye, I suppose you do. 'Tis a good thing you ran off from your master. I wish I had the courage to do the same." Craig drained his cup. "Well, I reckon it's time I be a going' back to me loft."

"Stay here with us tonight," offered Jonas. "We have a fine, big bed of pine straw and an extra blanket. There's no need for you to be wandering off into the dark of night." He winked. "We can drink some more tea and swap a few lies."

Craig smiled mischievously. "Aye. I reckon I can stay. And I have some stories that will curl your toes!"

11
INQUIRIES

Three Days Later

It was late afternoon and a cloudy day. It had been raining off and on since the sunrise. Jonas was seated on a stool beside the window. He was passing the time by watching squirrels playing in the nearby trees. It was obvious that he was quite bored.

"What do you see out there?" asked Justus as he tossed a fresh log onto the fire. "You have been staring out that window for hours now."

"Nothing but squirrels, rabbits, and birds. It is the same as every other day out here in the woods," Jonas answered. "There is nothing else to do but watch the world outside my window." He sighed wistfully. "It is just so boring out here, Justus. I can barely stand it."

"Would you rather be back in Baltimore City?" his brother teased. "With people chasing us all the long day and sometimes shooting at us?"

Jonas paused for a moment and then answered,

"Almost. At least we stayed on the move while we were there. There was always a place to go or a clue to investigate. I enjoyed this hiding out business for the first day or so, but now it is beginning to wear on me. If we do not leave this place soon, I may lose my mind."

Suddenly, Jonas saw movement near the edge of the trees. There was a flash of white cloth somewhere beyond the thick foliage. Seconds later Charity emerged from the woods, walking along the rocky path that led to the house.

"It's Charity!" exclaimed Jonas. "And she has our supper!"

Charity immediately spotted Jonas looking at her through the window. She smiled happily and waved. Jonas leapt from his chair and darted to the door. Justus joined him. They opened the door and warmly greeted their friend.

"Hello, outlaw fugitives," she declared, grinning happily. "I trust you are both warm and well-rested."

"A little too well-rested," declared Justus, closing the door. "My little brother has become bored unto madness ... or so he says."

She chuckled. "Well, perhaps the news that I bear will revive you both."

"You have discovered something?" asked Justus, his voice filled with eager anticipation.

"I did, indeed. Philip Morrison, the fellow I know who serves at the Treadway plantation, came into town this morning. He ate his mid-day meal at the tavern, and we had time for a brief conversation."

"And? What did he tell you?" asked Jonas impatiently.

"He told me that he knew your father and that he had been well-loved on the plantation. Indeed, he spoke very highly of Mr. Avery. He was beloved amongst all the servants and slaves."

Justus felt a great heaviness in his chest. "Charity, why are you speaking of our father in the past tense?"

She frowned. "Because I bear some bad news as well."

Justus' heart leapt into his throat. "Is he ... is he ... dead?"

Charity placed a reassuring hand on his arm. "No, Justus, your father is not dead, so far as I know. But he is no longer at the Treadway plantation. Phillip told me that Mr. Treadway's son sold your father's indenture about a month after he inherited the plantation. He is now somewhere up in the northern part of the county. Philip did not know the exact location."

Jonas stared forlornly at his brother. He stomped, obviously frustrated. "I knew it! I just knew it! This has all been for nothing! It is just another dead end!"

"Stop your pouting, Jonas," Charity scolded him. "You are being a bit overly dramatic. It is not as if your father has returned to England or been sent to sea. He is right down the road and only a few miles distant. You can walk to wherever he is in an afternoon."

"It's just so frustrating," responded Jonas woefully. "Just when it seemed we were nearing the finish of our quest, there arose yet another complication. Will this trail of disappointing clues never end?"

"They end when we find Papa," declared Justus harshly, his voice revealing some anger. "And he is worth both the search and the wait. Don't you agree?"

Jonas nodded, though he did not appear much consoled.

Justus turned to Charity. "We must put our minds

together and come up with a plan. How can we find out exactly where our Papa has gone?"

Charity turned to her basket. "No. First, we will see to supper and *then* we shall make a plan." She paused. "Oh! I almost forgot. I brought you a little something to help you pass the time here in your secret hideaway." She reached into her basket and then produced a worn deck of playing cards.

Jonas' face lit up with pleasure. "Charity, you are the best!"

❦

One Hour Later

"IT IS THE MOST SENSIBLE COURSE OF ACTION," declared Justus. "I must be the one to speak to Mr. Treadway. I could pose as a gentleman and visit him at his home. Once I am inside, I can sneak into his office and then search for the record of Papa's indenture and sale."

Jonas appeared skeptical. "Where will you get clothes for such an effort?" He chuckled. "You surely do not look like much of a gentleman. You look more like a lanky farm boy, straight out of the field. And I think that *you* must think you look older than you truly are." He rolled his eyes and then looked to Charity. "Just imagine! Justus ... the distinguished gentleman!"

"I could do it," growled Justus, his face reddening with angry embarrassment.

"But what about clothing? You would need an entire suit of fine clothes to masquerade as a young gentleman,"

Jonas challenged. He glanced around the empty cabin. "I see no fine menswear hereabouts."

"Charity could get me the clothing I need," retorted Justus. He turned to Charity. "Right?"

"Perhaps," she responded reluctantly. "I get plenty of shirts and stockings left behind in the tavern, and occasionally some breeches. But rarely has anyone ever left behind a coat or weskit. It would be difficult to find clothes to fit you."

"And what about your shoes?" asked Jonas, pointing to holes in Justus' black leather buckle shoes. "You would need brand-new ones, and likely new buckles, as well. Surely Charity does not have any men's shoes to give you."

"Oh, all right, then!" Justus surrendered angrily. "So, tell me your bright idea! How do you suggest we get access to Mr. Treadway's records?"

"That's easy," Jonas answered confidently. "We get them the same way we got those records from the hospital back in Baltimore. We sneak onto the plantation under the cover of darkness, break into the house, and then find our way to his study. Then we can search through is records until we find what we are looking for."

"How do you propose to see those records in the darkness?" challenged Justus. "There were streetlamps in Baltimore that lit up the room at night. You are suggesting invading the master's house on a huge plantation in the dark of night. We could not light a candle. People would see the glow through the window. What you are saying makes no sense. I say we go with my plan."

"But what are you going to purchase a clothes and shoes with, Justus? Happy thoughts?" Jonas mocked. "Because we are out of money!"

Back and forth they went, bickering and fighting, each of them growing angrier and angrier with every word. Finally, Charity had endured all that she could stand. She stood up from the table and stomped an angry foot.

"Enough! Both of you!"

Silence instantly descended upon the room. The brothers stared, utterly shocked, at their female friend. They had never before seen such an emotional outburst from her.

"I will not listen to any more of your juvenile arguing. Frankly, I find it tiresome." She paused. "And, besides, it is quite unnecessary. You are both complicating matters that are altogether uncomplicated."

Sensing that she had their complete attention, she fluffed her petticoat and then returned to her seat in a most ladylike manner.

Justus cleared his throat. He asked with stunned politeness, "Do you have a solution, Charity?"

She nodded. "I do."

Justus smiled uncomfortably. "What, then, do you propose?"

"First," she began, "I want the two of you to immediately change your manner of thinking. I fear that you have both been fugitives from the law for far too long. Your minds automatically incline toward devious thoughts and illegal activities. There is absolutely no need for masquerading as someone you are not." She glared somewhat angrily at Jonas. "And no one is breaking into anyone's home. You must remember that these people are neighbors. I know these folk. I'll not have you sneaking in and pilfering through their possessions."

"So how, then, do we find out where Papa went?" asked Jonas in a trembling voice.

"We simply ask," replied Charity. "We walk up to the man's door, give it a knock, and then ask politely."

Jonas turned to Justus. He appeared perplexed. "Do you think that could work?"

Justus shrugged. "I reckon it *could* work. Seems a bit simple to me, though."

"Of course, it will work!" exclaimed Charity in exasperation. "Not everyone in this world is evil, or your enemy, or chasing after you. There are still good folk who are willing and able to help. I do not know Albert Treadway all that well, but I am reasonably certain that he is a gentleman."

"But we cannot possibly go out in public," protested Jonas. "Someone might see us and then call the sheriff."

She smiled. "I agree. You cannot go. Instead, I will go for you."

"*You* will go for us?" echoed Justus. He shook his head. "I cannot allow you to take such a risk for us."

"There is no risk. The Treadways are neighbors and customers at the tavern. I have served their table many times. They pose no threat to me. I will go to young Mr. Treadway, explain the circumstance, and then ask for his help. Surely, he will tell me where you father has gone."

Jonas nodded reluctantly. "She is right, Justus. This is a perfect mission for Charity. We have to trust her instincts."

Justus sighed and nodded. "Charity, you are correct, of course ... and most wise. And we are most humbled by and grateful for your offer. When will you go?"

"Sunday. The tavern is closed, and I do not have to work. It is a perfect day to pay a call and make an inquiry."

"Will you go alone?" Justus asked, still quite concerned.

"No. I will have Craig drive me. He can use one of the carriages or wagons for rent from the livery."

"Won't that cost some money?" asked Jonas.

"No. The livery master allows Craig to use his horses and vehicles as he has need." She grinned. "Do not worry. I have the mission and the plan well in hand." She stood. "But now I must depart. The hour grows late, and I have work to do this evening. The tavern is certain to be full tonight."

Justus and Jonas stood respectfully. They helped Charity clear the table and place all of the dishes and eating utensils back into her basket.

"Thank you for that fine supper, Charity," declared Jonas. He winked. "I look forward to an even better breakfast tomorrow."

Charity reached over and pinched his plump cheek. "And I look forward to bringing it to you." She stepped to the door and opened the latch. Turning, she said, "Good evening, gentlemen. I shall see you tomorrow."

"Goodbye, Charity," declared the Avery brothers in unison.

She bowed gracefully, opened the door, and then stepped outside. Justus closed the door behind her.

"What now?" asked Jonas.

Justus retrieved the deck of cards from his pocket. "How about a game of cards?"

Jonas grinned happily. "You read my mind."

Noon the Next Day

"WHERE CAN SHE BE?" MOANED JONAS. "THE DAY IS half-way done and I'm starving."

"I am not worried about hunger," Justus said. "I am worried about Charity. She has never been late before. Something *must* be wrong."

"What could possibly be wrong?" asked Jonas.

Justus shook his head. His look was grim. "I don't know. That is what worries me so."

Suddenly there was a knock at the door. Justus turned immediately toward the sound. Jonas jumped as if he had been shot, the unexpected sound had frightened him so.

"Good heavens!" Justus exclaimed. "Why did Charity slip up on us like that? She usually announces her arrival."

Justus ignored his brother and immediately darted to the door. Anxious to see Charity, he opened it quickly to welcome their visitor. His countenance fell somewhat when he saw who was standing outside. It was Charity's cousin, the stable boy, Craig MacLellan. He was carrying a linen market sack over his shoulder. The sack was bulging and filled with cargo.

"Hello, Craig," Justus greeted him in a monotone. He glanced past the boy toward the pathway that led toward the woods.

"She's not here," Craig declared, seemingly reading Justus' thoughts. He stepped into the house. "Charity did not think it safe to leave town today."

"Why?" demanded Justus. What has happened?"

Craig removed his tricorn cocked hat and then placed it on the peg beside the door. He turned to the brothers.

"There's a strange fellow in town. He's been askin' lots of questions."

"What manner of questions?" asked Jonas.

He sighed hesitantly. "Questions about the two of you."

Craig reached into his pocket and removed a piece of paper. He handed it to Justus. It was a handbill identical to the ones that they had seen in Baltimore. It bore their image and the announcement of the reward for their capture. Jonas peered over his brother's shoulder in disbelief. He snatched the paper out of Justus' hand and waved it frantically in the air.

"Sledge has found us!" Jonas exclaimed. "The dogs will be coming for certain!"

"I saw no dogs," confessed Craig. "There was only one fellow. A young man he was, barely older than all of us. He was travelin' on horseback. He's been posting these handbills all over town and making inquiries in most of the taverns and stores. I was in the *Sleeping Bear* when he talked to Charity and the other serving girls."

"A young fellow, you say?" confirmed Justus.

Craig nodded. "Aye. He has blonde hair and blue eyes. And he speaks like a Marylander from near the coast. He's from Baltimore, I suspect, or someplace close by."

Justus rubbed his chin thoughtfully. He looked at his brother and shook his head. He appeared perplexed. "He does not sound familiar to me. Do you recall anyone who looks like that, Jonas?"

The younger brother shook his head. "Not at all."

"He is likely a hired man," suggested Craig. "It sounds as if this Sledge fellow really wants to find you lads. I'll bet he's plenty frustrated after you gave him the slip in Baltimore. It would be easy enough for him to hire some men and then send them out into the countryside to search the villages and towns and post these handbills."

Justus nodded thoughtfully. "That would, indeed, explain his arrival. Surely there is no way that anyone knows we are here. How could they?"

Craig nodded in agreement. "No one but Charity and I know you are here. I am certain of that."

Justus took the handbill from Jonas and examined it once more. "Still, this is proof positive that our pursuers are still after us. Sledge wants us badly."

"And he wants our father, as well. We *must* find Papa first." Jonas turned to Craig. "You say Charity talked to this fellow?"

"She did. Over breakfast this mornin'. She served him."

Jonas' eyes narrowed. "What did she tell him?"

Craig grinned mischievously. "Well, as I told you, the fellow has blonde hair and eyes as blue as the summer sky. He is a terribly handsome lad, all dressed in buckskin and a linen hunting frock. Charity simply could not help herself, poor lass. She gave in to his charm and beauty and told him everythin'. She told him what you had for supper last night and then drew him a map to this house. She even gave him a kiss after."

"Liar!" hissed Jonas angrily, his face beet-red. "This is nothing to joke about, Craig."

Justus and Craig both erupted in uncontrolled laughter. Sensing Jonas' frustration, Craig walked over to younger lad and gave him a reassuring pat on the shoulder.

"Worry not, Jonas. Our beloved Charity told him nothin', of course. She denied ever havin' seen or heard of either of you. Still, she felt it was too risky to be a bringin' you any more hot meals. You must admit ... it may seem a bit odd for her to be haulin' baskets filled with hot food out the back door each day. If this fellow were to see her it could make him suspect something was afoot, to be sure. That is why she sent me in her stead."

"That was good thinking on her part," agreed Justus. "Anyone paying attention to her comings and goings *could* become suspicious. In fact, the cooks and other servers may already suspect something. We must be more careful going forward."

"But what about food?" challenged the every-hungry Jonas. "We are trapped here for at least two more days, perhaps more. What are we supposed to eat?"

"Fear not, young Mr. Avery. Charity had a plan, wise lass that she is. She gave me a couple of your coins and then sent me to purchase some supplies for you." He removed the linen sack from his shoulder, placed it on the table, and began to remove the items inside. "I have five pounds of potatoes, a horn of salt, a large sack of dried peas, six small loaves of bread, and some dried beef. You should be able to get by with all that until Sunday."

"That will do nicely," affirmed Justus. "It is more than enough for the two of us." His eyes twinkled. "Perhaps even enough for three."

"That's what I was a thinkin'." Craig grinned happily. He tossed his empty sack across his shoulder and then ambled toward the door. "I'll be back around sunset. Have a pot of tea on to brew. The baker's wife has hired me to bring in a load of wood this afternoon. I will see if I might rustle up some sweet biscuits for tonight's dessert."

Justus waved to his young friend. "We shall be waiting for you with some hot stew and a deck of cards."

12

GOOD NEWS, BAD NEWS

Sunday Afternoon

Charity stood in front of the towering front door of the Treadway house. She smoothed her petticoats and checked her gown for loose threads or lint. She tucked a wandering strand of hair back inside her bonnet. Satisfied that she was presentable, she took a deep breath, reached up and took hold of the iron door knocker, and then rapped it against the door three times. She held her breath in anticipation as she waited for someone to answer the door. She was just about to strike the knocker again when the latch clicked, and the door opened inward. An attractive, bright-eyed young girl greeted her.

"Good afternoon," said the girl. "How may I help you?"

Charity inhaled an apprehensive breath. "I am Charity MacLellan. I have come to speak to Mr. Albert Treadway about a personal matter."

The girl smiled. "I am Elizabeth Treadway, his eldest daughter. Is my father expecting you?"

"No, Miss Treadway. I sincerely apologize for arriving unannounced and on a Sunday. I only do so because the matter is urgent. My inquiry will only take a moment, I assure you."

The girl opened the door wide and then stepped to one side. "Of course. Please come in, Miss MacLellan." She motioned to an adjacent room. "If you wait in the parlor, I will fetch my father for you."

"Thank you, Miss Treadway."

The ever-smiling girl nodded. "You are most welcome. And please call me Libby."

Charity smiled, feeling somewhat less nervous and intimidated. "Thank you, Libby."

The charming girl departed, leaving Charity alone in the parlor. She stood awkwardly in front of a long French sofa. She was not certain whether or not she should sit. A few minutes later a handsome, middle-aged man stepped into the room. His hair was light brown and streaked with gray. It was pulled back into a braided queue. He wore an immaculate suit made of fine, dark gray linen.

"Hello," he greeted Charity. He appeared somewhat puzzled. "Do I know you, Miss?"

Charity smiled uncomfortably and nodded. "Perhaps so, Mr. Treadway. I am Charity MacLellan. I serve at *The Sleeping Bear*. You have dined at my table a time or two."

"Ah, yes," he acknowledged, still looking confused. "I remember you now. An able tavern servant you are. But what brings you to my home today, Miss MacLellan? 'Tis a bit improper for a servant girl to call upon a gentleman in his home."

Charity's face flushed red. She was very embarrassed. "Indeed, it is, sir. I apologize for the impropriety. But I have not come on my own behalf. I have called upon you to make a simple inquiry for some acquaintances of mine. They are looking for their father and believe that you may know his whereabouts."

He cocked his head to one side, clearly intrigued. "Such an inquiry sounds most odd. What is their father's name?"

"Jeremiah Avery. He is a cobbler. I believe that he was indentured to your father. I heard from one of your workers that you sold his indenture sometime last year. I simply ask that you relate to me his current location."

Mr. Treadway nodded. "I remember Jeremiah. He was a well-mannered fellow and fondly regarded amongst the servants. When I assumed responsibility for this plantation, I did not see the need to retain a cobbler in my employ. Indeed, I thought from the start that my father was acting foolishly when he purchased the man's indenture." He frowned and shook his head. "But I have come to regret letting him go. I did not realize how valuable Jeremiah's work was to our farm production." He cocked his head in curiosity. "Who did you say is looking for him?"

Charity answered, "Some acquaintances of mine."

"Such a vague answer." Mr. Treadway narrowed his gaze at Charity. He raised a single eyebrow in intrigue. "Why have they not come to inquire themselves?"

"Because their circumstance will not allow it, sir." She sighed. "It is far too difficult to explain, and the story is much too long to tell."

The gentleman chuckled and then shook his head. "What an interesting day this has become! I feared that I would suffer yet another Sunday afternoon of tedious reading. Now a lovely tavern girl has come to my home in search of an indentured cobbler for some anonymous acquaintances." He smiled. "Young lady, I believe that you have just rescued me from an afternoon of boredom. Now I *must* hear your story."

"Please, sir. I must not waste your time. If you will just tell me the location of Mr. Avery, then I will beg your leave."

"Nonsense!" He motioned politely to the sofa. "Please sit, and I will have my Libby fetch us some tea and biscuits. Then you must tell me this interesting story."

A Short Time Later

Mr. Treadway shook his head in wonder and disbelief. "What a marvelous tale! It is hard to believe that two young boys have seen and experienced so much difficulty and grief in their short lifetimes. The story of their sea journey was both tragic and captivating. I think that I should like to meet these intrepid young lads." He paused thoughtfully. "Of course, as I, myself, am the master of a plantation, I cannot condone the actions of your friends. 'Tis no small thing to run away from one's indenture. It is a criminal act."

"As well I know it, sir," affirmed Charity sullenly. "I, too, am an indentured servant."

He nodded thoughtfully. "Still, I can understand their motivation. Surely both they and their father have suffered grave injustices." He eyed her admirably. "So, you have been helping these lads, actually hiding them all this time?"

She nodded. "Yes, sir. They are good friends. I am honored to help them in their quest."

He cast a curious glance at Charity. "And all this talk of treasure and the men pursuing it ... do you think any of it is true? Might such a treasure truly exist? And if so, why would their father remain confined in indentured servitude? Why not simply purchase his own freedom?"

"The boys believe it is because he has been saving his money for them. He wants to reunite with them and then purchase some land of their own. It was the dream of owning land that brought them to America. Therefore, until his sons find him, he has chosen to remain silent." She shrugged. "Plus, he is likely afraid that suddenly producing a sum of gold and silver would attract much unwanted attention. Men will kill for money. That is what Justus and Jonas surmise, at least."

He nodded. "They are correct. That makes as much sense as any other explanation." He sighed thoughtfully. "Actually, I can think of no other explanation."

"So, will you help them? Will you help my friends reunite with their long-lost father?"

He chuckled and then nodded respectfully to Charity. "Of course, I will. 'Twould be an honor to do so." He stood. "If you will excuse me, I will retire to my study and consult my records. I shall have the information for you shortly."

"Thank you, Mr. Treadway."

He smiled happily. "It is my distinct pleasure, Miss MacLellan."

He bowed to her and then turned and strode swiftly from the room.

❧

THE CARRIAGE JOSTLED AND BOUNCED ALONG THE DUSTY roadway toward town. Craig expertly guided the rig along the smoothest route possible, careful to avoid any large holes or ruts.

"So, the man just up and told you everythin'?" marveled Craig in disbelief.

Charity nodded. "He did, indeed." She held up a slip of yellowed paper. "He gave me the name of Mr. Avery's new master, along with the name and location of his plantation."

"Did he ask you any questions?"

"A few," admitted Charity. "Actually, he demanded to hear the Avery boys' entire story. I had to tell him everything from start to finish. That is what took me so long."

Craig pondered her words. "Do you reckon he will call the sheriff on them?"

Charity shook her head. "Certainly not. He was most sympathetic to the plight of the Avery boys. Indeed, he wished them well. As he is a gentleman, I will take him at his word."

"Gentleman!" grunted Craig, his voice filled with sarcasm. "Could he not be just like the gentlemen who declared us orphans and then sold us into servitude? Or the gentleman who now has his men and his dogs chasing after Justus and Jonas?" He shook his head, scowling. "You cannot trust rich folk Charity. That is simply the way of things."

"I believe Mr. Treadway to be sincere." She held up the paper once more. "And I believe that this is the evidence of his sincerity."

"We shall see," retorted Craig, his tone remaining doubtful.

Minutes later they drove into the outskirts of Upper Marlborough. Craig guided the rig over a small wooden bridge and then turned down the main thoroughfare that went through the center of the village. The route to the livery stable took them past *The Sleeping Bear*. As they drove by the tavern, they noticed two men standing on the front porch of the establishment. They were speaking to Hannah, one of the cooks who worked in the kitchen. One was an older, foul-looking fellow. The other was thin and somewhat haggard. He was obviously the other man's servant or assistant.

"Who are those fellows?" asked Craig. "Don't they know that *The Sleepin' Bear* is closed on Sunday?"

Charity shrugged. "Likely they are not from around here."

She glanced back over her shoulder and observed the men. Suddenly, Hannah pointed directly at her and Craig. Both men turned and started at them as they rode down the street.

"What is going on over there?" she wondered aloud. Her voice was low and foreboding. "Why are they concerned with us?"

"What? Is something wrong?" queried Craig, peering over his shoulder. He, too, saw Hannah and the men looking at them. "Why are Hannah and those men so interested in us?"

Charity shook her head slowly. "I do not know."

As she turned to once more face forward in her seat, she noticed a wagon parked in front of the mercantile, directly across the street from the tavern. Inside the wagon bed were several cages, and inside those cages were roughly a dozen sleeping hounds.

She gasped. “Oh, heavens!”

“What is it?” asked Craig, confused.

She spun around in the wagon seat and pointed forward. “Go quickly! Do not stop at the livery! Take me over the bridge and drop me at the end of the path.”

“Why? What is wrong, Charity?” he demanded.

She explained, “Those men ... they have a wagon load of dogs with them.”

Craig’s eyes widened in horror. “It must be the men who are after Justus and Jonas!”

She nodded slowly. “It is Sledge.” She nodded forward. “Take me to the path. I must get to the lads and warn them.”

Craig shook his head. “No,” he declared. He pulled on the reins and spoke soothingly to the horses. Their speed decreased slightly.

“What are you doing?” demanded Charity. “Why are you slowing down?”

“If we look as if we are fleeing the town that will make them even more suspicious. We must go straightway to the livery. Once there, you can go out the back and then cut through the pine thicket and head cross-country to the hideout. Do you know the way through the woods?”

She nodded. “I have traveled that way before. There is small trail, isn’t there?”

“Yes. It is an old deer trail. It will take you directly to the lane that leads to your old house. You must warn the

Avery boys. I will follow soon behind you. I will saddle two horses and then make my way to the hideout."

"You cannot give them your master's horses," she protested earnestly.

"I do not intend to. I will give them my own horse. They can use it to make their escape." He grinned. "The second horse is for me to return to the livery."

"You intend to send them on your skinny old nag?" she exclaimed, raising an eyebrow in uncertainty. "I doubt that ancient mare of yours can make it very far."

Craig was much offended. "You will learn differently, and soon." He pointed to the note in her hand. "Where is Mr. Avery now? Where will the fellows be going?"

"He is at the *Willow Grove* plantation, up near Collington."

"That is only ten miles to the north." He nodded proudly. "Old Ruth can make it that far, and at least another five miles more if needs be."

Charity rolled her eyes. "I doubt it."

"Do not doubt me, Charity. I know what my own horse can do."

Seconds later he guided the rig through the double doors of the livery. He tugged the reins and brought the team to a quick stop.

"Go now!" Craig urged. "I will be along as quickly as I can."

Charity did not respond verbally. She merely nodded and then leapt from the wagon seat. She disappeared like a flash through the rear door.

Thirty Minutes Later

"Are you sure it was Sledge?" asked Justus as he hurriedly shoved his meager belongings into his haversack.

Charity nodded. "Yes. He was a dour, evil-looking older man accompanied by a scrawny fellow. And they had a wagon filled with dogs."

"That is Sledge, for sure," affirmed Jonas in a foreboding tone. "How on earth did he find us?"

"He was talking to Hannah, one of our cooks. I am not certain, but I imagine that she said something to the younger fellow who came to town and posted the reward notices with your image on them. She likely told him about the food that I have been taking out each morning and evening." She shrugged. "He must have figured everything out and then informed his employer."

"And now Sledge has come here to get us!" added Jonas angrily. "Hannah betrayed you and us at the same time. No doubt she has received a nice reward in silver and copper." He scowled. "One day I shall have some words with your cook-friend. But for now, how will we escape Sledge and his hounds?"

"Craig is on the way now with a horse for you. You will take it and ride to your father. You shall be with him by suppertime this very night." She smiled encouragingly. "I know that he will be so excited."

"Where is Papa now?" asked Justus as he continued packing his belongings and gear.

"He is at *Willow Creek*, a tobacco plantation up near Collington. It is the home of a gentleman named Walter Bowie." She handed Justus the paper given to her by Mr. Treadway. "The Bowies are very influential people in the northern part of the county. Their plantation should be easy enough to find."

Outside they heard hooves pounding upon the path, signaling the approach of horses. Justus looked out the window and soon spotted Craig emerging from the trees.

"He is here." Justus turned to his brother. "Do you have everything?"

Jonas grinned. "It is easy to pack when you don't own anything a'tall."

The door opened and Craig entered quickly. He was winded and appeared troubled.

"There is no time to waste, lads! I saw those men head-ing' to the livery just before I left. They are hot on my trail, no doubt. You fellows need to get goin'!" He motioned with his thumb over his shoulder. "I have your horse waitin' outside. Her name is Ruth. She is old and a bit slow, and a little bit deaf, but she is determined. She will get you to where you are goin'. Take good care of her. She is my very own mount." He winked. "And I expect her back in a day or two."

Justus nodded. "I shall return your animal as soon as possible. Which way should we go?"

"You need to take the creek to the east. Keep the horse in the water at all times. 'Tis no more than ankle deep most of the way. The water will leave no evidence of your passing and it will conceal your scent from the dogs. The creek will take you all the way to the northern road. That highway will take you straight into Collington. Meanwhile, I will see if I can throw them off your trail."

"How will you do that?" asked Jonas.

Craig grinned mischievously. "Let's just say that I will be a sendin' them on a bit of a wild goose chase."

Justus smiled and extended his hand to his friend. They shook. "We cannot thank you enough for all that you have done." He turned his eyes to Charity. "Both of you."

"It has been an honor and a pleasure." Charity smiled warmly. "Now go! There is no time to waste. Go and find your Papa. And let us know when you are settled and safe."

She hugged both boys. They grabbed their bags and blanket rolls and then headed out the door. Charity and Craig followed. Justus and Jonas mounted the old mare quickly and then disappeared into the woods near the creek.

"Do you think they will find him?" asked Craig solemnly.

Charity sighed. "I pray so."

13
TWO SCOUNDRELS AND A GENTLEMAN

Craig MacLellan left the secret house in the woods and headed back toward town. Minutes later he led his horse from the forest path onto the well-traveled roadway. He rounded the first bend in the road and immediately encountered two men riding in a wagon. It was Abram Sledge and John Bailey, along with their caged hounds.

"*Here we go,*" Craig thought silently to himself. "*Time to send these two scoundrels back to Virginia.*" He urged his horse forward.

"You, there!" called Abram Sledge. "I require your assistance!"

Craig nonchalantly headed in their direction. He was in no hurry. He smiled and nodded respectfully, tipping his hat. "Of course, sir. How may I help you?"

"We are travelers from Frederick County, Virginia, and in need of some information."

"You fellows are a far piece from home." He pointed to the dogs in the wagon bed. "What have you come here for, to sell some hounds? I doubt anyone has use for such animals 'round here. Not many men hereabouts use them for hunting. We use our skill and cunning."

Sledge shook his head. "No, young fellow, we are not selling these hounds. Rather, we are looking for a young woman by the name of Charity MacLellan. Do you happen to know her?"

Craig grinned and nodded. "I should say that I do. Charity is my beloved cousin, and a kindly, dear soul. I reckon she's my favorite person in this whole wide world."

The man gave something of a start and appeared to be completely surprised. "She is your *cousin*?" he asked, his voice almost cracking.

"Aye, sir. Charity and I are blood kin. She's actually more of a sister to me, truth be told. She's taken fine care of me these past few years ... much more so than my own master ever has." He narrowed his eyes and eyed the dogs with suspicion. "Say ... why would you two be a comin' after my Charity with a pack of hounds?" He shook an angry fist. "She is no outlaw! She is a fine, upstandin' young woman!"

"Calm down, boy. The hounds are not for her," promised Sledge. "I simply need to talk to her. Do you know where Miss MacLellan has gone?"

Craig nonchalantly signaled over his shoulder with his thumb. "She is out at the old MacLellan homeplace and doing a little cleanin', I suspect. I just left there, and it is quite the mess, believe you me! Those two fellows she allowed to stay out there last week have gone and tore up her mama's old house."

Sledge's eyes grew wide. "*Two* fellows you say?" he echoed excitedly. "Young lads, were they?"

"Aye. Mysterious fellows, they were. Justus and Jonas were their names. They were an odd lot, though ... always talkin' about bein' runaways from Virginia, and lookin' for their papa, and seekin' a lost treasure. 'Twas all a bunch of nonsense if you ask me. I think they made it all up just to impress my cousin, Charity."

"You spoke to them personally ... the Avery boys, I mean?" Sledge clarified. He was on the edge of his wagon seat with excitement.

"Of course, I did! And I ate supper with 'em a time or two." He smiled a toothy grin as he rubbed his belly. "I've never been one to miss out on a free meal."

The other fellow, who was, no doubt, the lackey John Bailey, began tapping Sledge on the shoulder. After a few taps Sledge became quite annoyed.

"Please stop doing that, John! I am on the verge of finding these runaways and you are interrupting me!"

John Bailey leaned in close and whispered something to Sledge. A look of realization washed across Sledge's face. He turned and glared accusingly at Craig.

"Did we not, less than two hours ago, see you ride through town in a wagon with Miss MacLellan by your side?"

Craig nodded. "Aye. I told you. She is my cousin. I took her this mornin' to visit a widow-woman down by the old mill. We were just comin' back into town when we saw you fellows at the tavern and talkin' to Hannah, the cook. Charity took off runnin' just as soon as we got back to the livery. She looked plenty worried, believe me."

Craig suddenly displayed his own look of realization and understanding. It was a superb job of acting on his part. He snapped his fingers and then pointed to the hounds.

"Hey, wait a minute! I know who you fellows are now! You are old man Sledge and his boot-lickin' tattletale, John Bailey!" He pointed to the dogs. "And those are your no-good hounds!" He snickered. "I hear tell they can't find a chicken in a barnyard."

Both men's faces turned blood-red. Sledge shouted, "Why, you disrespectful little rascal! I'll not be addressed in such a manner by the likes of you!"

Craig flashed a huge, disarming smile. "I meant no offense, sirs. I was just repeatin' what Justus and Jonas said. I mean, that was how they described you in their very own words." He shook his head, feigning disbelief. "Them two claimed all along they had two men and a pack of hounds after them, but I never before believed them." He chuckled. "And to think that they were a tellin' me the truth the whole long time! I reckon I'll have to be eatin' some of my words now. Yes, sir!"

Mr. Sledge appeared to be somewhat appeased. The red color in his cheeks diminished. He asked, "Why do you think Miss MacLellan was in such a hurry when she left you?"

Craig explained, "She wanted to help cover those boys' tracks and keep you from catchin' 'em, of course." He winked. "I think she was a bit partial to the oldest one."

Sledge cut his eyes at John Bailey and then turned back to Craig. "When did you see them last?"

"Three days ago. No ... wait ... it four days ago, actually. It was right before they lit out."

"Lit out?" Sledge echoed excitedly.

Craig nodded. "Yes, sir. They were hoofin' it westward back to old Virginny."

"Back to Virginia?" clarified Sledge, a look of disbelief on his face. "Why would they go back to Virginia?"

"They told me they found a letter down in Baltimore sayin' that their old pappy had gone west to the Kentucky Country. So, naturally, they lit out on his trail." He paused, shaking his head. "But I surely hope you catch them thievin' boys. Lord knows they have it comin' to them. They be a slippery pair, that's for sure."

Sledge eyed him with suspicion. "Why? I thought they were your friends. What did they do to you?"

"The younger one stole from me, that's what! I was playin' a game of cards with his brother and the little cuss robbed me blind. Took every penny from my purse, he did!"

Sledge pointed his finger at Craig. "So, let me get this straight. You are telling me that the Avery lads have been hiding out somewhere in these woods, all the while assisted by your cousin?"

Craig nodded. "Yes, sir."

"And they departed four days ago for the Kentucky country?"

Craig nodded. "Yes, sir. Just as sure as my name be Craig MacLellan! They are walkin' to a place called Martin's Station, and then on through the gap into Kentucky." He paused. "Though I did hear the older one say that he had some unfinished business just across the river. He said he had been a charmin' his old master's daughter and that he planned on stealin' her away to Kentucky with him."

Sledge's head spun. He locked eyes with John Bailey.

"Good Lord! They are going after Miss Drusilla! They intend to kidnap her! We must return home immediately!"

He reached into his pocket and retrieved a small Spanish silver coin. He tossed the coin to Craig. "Here is a reward for your troubles, young man."

Craig removed his hat and nodded humbly. "I am happy to oblige, sir. I wish you both safe travels." He paused. "And your hounds."

The two men ignored his well-wishes. John Bailey tugged on one of the reins, quickly turned the rig around in the middle of the highway, and then immediately headed back toward town. Craig grinned happily as he watched them go, disappearing around a bend in the road. He admired the shiny silver coin in the palm of his hand.

He declared happily, "And I thank you kindly, Mr. Sledge. Your contribution to my supper fund is much appreciated."

He gave a celebratory flip of the coin, caught it in his outstretched hand, and then tucked it safely away inside the pocket of his weskit. He clucked at his horse and then followed the wagon toward town at a leisurely pace. As he rode, he glanced upward toward the clear, blue sky.

"Forgive me, Lord, for the bucket full of lies that I just told." He winked skyward. "But you know well enough that they were for all the right reasons."

❧

CHARITY'S HEART WAS HEAVY. ONCE MORE SHE WAS alone. The old, abandoned house was once again shrouded in emptiness and silence. The laughter and fellowship that she had enjoyed with the Averys was no more. Her friends were gone. They were on the way to be reunited with their long-lost father. No doubt their coming days would be filled with great happiness and joy.

She was happy for them ... very much so. Still, she could not help but suffer the numbing pain of their absence. She had enjoyed providing for them, spending time with them, and talking with them. She missed them terribly, even though she had only known them for a mere two weeks.

She shook her head and then marveled aloud to herself, "Has it truly only been that long? Just two weeks?"

Justus and Jonas Avery did not feel like short-term, fleeting friends to her. Rather, they felt like friends for a lifetime. She supposed that was why their absence caused her such emptiness and pain. She hoped to see them again someday but, at the same time, doubted that they would ever return. Indeed, why would they?

Charity attempted to overcome her loneliness by focusing on her work. Her family's old home needed a thorough cleaning. The Avery brothers had taken relatively good care of the place during their sojourn there, so there was not much to do. Still, the place needed a good going-over. The glass windows needed cleaning and the floors needed to be swept. She also had to scoop the ashes and coals from the fireplace and replenish the supply of firewood. She wanted the house to be clean and ready for her next retreat into the woods.

Her first order of business, though, was to disassemble the brothers' makeshift bed. She wanted to remove their improvised mattress of pine needles and leaves. The debris from the forest floor, though it made a fine bed, was quite messy. She was also concerned about the presence of insects in the bedding. She reached down and took hold of a folded blanket that had served as Justus' pillow and gave it a shake. When she did a small scrap of paper floated to the floor near her feet.

"What's this?" she mumbled to herself as she retrieved the paper.

She turned it over and discovered that it was a note. Curiously, she noticed that it was addressed to her. She unfolded it and began to read.

Dearest Charity,

I sense that the time of our departure is drawing near. I am excited by the prospect of finding our father, yet I am also saddened because finding him will mean that we will be leaving you and this wonderful house. It has been a much needed and welcomed place of refuge for us. You ministered to Jonas and me in our time of greatest need. For that we will always be in your debt.

I know full well that finding Father will not mean the end of our difficulties. There remains our status as runaways. We are still fugitives from the Virginia authorities. We may yet be arrested and returned to Frederick County. There is also the matter of our father's indentured servitude. Even when we find him, I am not certain that he or we will be truly free. There remain so many questions and uncertainties. Still, in the midst of all of our troubles, you have been there for us. You housed us, fed us, and befriended us. You showed us kindness and grace that we in no way deserved. You have been our beacon of hope in a very dark time in our lives.

Please know that, even as we go forth into the world on our own, you will remain in our hearts and our thoughts. No matter what the future holds, we will always have the cherished memo-

ries of you, our dear friend, Charity MacLellan. I pray that, one day, we may be able to repay our debt to you and return unto you the generosity that you have shown us. Until that day comes, I wish you all the best.

Your Humble Servant and Friend,

Justus Avery

Charity choked back the tears as she folded the paper and then tucked it into her pocket. She sighed deeply and declared, "Someday, Justus, I *will* see you both again. I just know it!"

Mid-Afternoon

THE AVERY BROTHERS HAD BEEN ON HORSEBACK FOR almost four hours. Craig had provided them with perfect directions. They followed the creek eastward for almost two miles until it intersected with a highway that ran north and south. They turned left and headed toward the village of Collington. They maintained a slow pace, careful not to tire out Craig's ancient mare. Twice they stopped to rest and water the horse and ask for directions to Mr. Walter Bowie's *Willow Creek* plantation. The local folk were friendly and helpful.

At long last they reached their destination. They rode along a lovely, tree-lined, shaded driveway. A large, white plantation house was just coming into view when they spied a simple sign dangling from a post along the side of the lane. It read, "*Willow Creek*."

"This is the place," declared Jonas with a sigh. "Our Papa is here."

"We hope," responded Justus, inhaling a deep, thoughtful breath. "Surely his indenture has not been sold yet again."

"Lord, I hope not!" groaned Jonas. "He has already been through enough." He hesitated a moment and then asked, "Are you certain that we can just ride up to the front door and knock? Shouldn't we scout the place first and look for possible danger?"

Justus shook his head. "I doubt there is any danger here."

"Well, I still don't like it," grumbled Jonas. "We have no notion of what we are getting into." He pointed to some servants working in the nearby fields. "There are indentures and slaves all over this plantation. Their master might help us but, then again, he might just turn us in to the local law. Rewards make men do terrible, selfish things. It is a mighty big risk, Justus."

Justus glanced over his shoulder at his brother. "It is a risk worth taking if it will get us to our father."

Jonas smiled hopefully and nodded. "You are right, of course. I cannot wait to see him."

They emerged from the lane onto a circular driveway that surrounded a lovely front lawn. Justus guided their tired old horse toward the front of the house, bringing her to a stop in front of a hitching post. Both lads climbed down and then Justus secured the horse's reins to the post. They trudged slowly toward the house, knocking the dust from their clothing and doing the best they could to make themselves presentable.

They climbed a flight of stone steps that led up to the wide front porch. There was large set of oak double-doors at the very center of the house. Justus led the way. They walked boldly to the doors, lifted the knocker, and then rapped it soundly against the brass plate. Seconds later a very distinguished-looking, middle-aged African fellow opened the right-side door. He was dressed in an immaculate black linen suit with a white neck sock, shirt, and stockings. Justus immediately assumed that the man was a slave.

The servant bowed slightly at the waist. "How may I be of service to you gentlemen?"

Justus removed his tricorn cocked hat and held it respectfully to his chest. "Good afternoon, sir. My name is Justus Avery. This is my brother, Jonas. Might we have a word with Mr. Bowie? It is regarding a most urgent matter."

"Mr. Bowie is visiting at his brother's house, just over the ridge. However, I am expecting him to return at any moment. Would you care to wait for him in his drawing room?"

Justus nodded. "That would be fine, sir. You are most kind to offer."

"Please follow me."

The boys stepped inside the house as the servant closed the door behind them. He led them down a wide hallway to a large office. The majesty of the drawing room took the boys' breath. It was filled with furniture made of mahogany and cherry. There were shiny, red silk curtains on the windows and colorful Oriental rugs on the floor. Every wall was lined with books. It seemed like there were thousands of them. It was difficult for the brothers to even imagine that so many books existed, much less inside a single room.

The servant motioned to two maroon-colored leather chairs. "Please make yourselves comfortable. Would you gentlemen like some tea while you wait?"

Justus nodded. "Yes, that would be wonderful. We are very tired from traveling. Tea would be most refreshing."

The dark-skinned man smiled. "Might you be hungry, as well?"

"Indeed, we are, sir," chirped Jonas hopefully, rubbing his belly.

The fellow's smile grew wider. "I shall see if Miss Mabel might fix you a little something. Please wait here and make yourself at home."

A few minutes later the man returned with a platter that contained a teapot and two cups, a bowl of sugar, a cup of cream, a plate piled high with sandwiches, and two shiny, red apples. He placed it on a small serving table near a large window that overlooked the gardens.

The servant bowed respectfully. "Enjoy your refreshments, gentlemen. I shall send Mr. Bowie to see you the moment that he returns."

"Might we have a look at some of these books?" inquired Justus. "Mr. Bowie's library is most impressive."

The man smiled and nodded. "Of course. Master Bowie prides himself on his collection and enjoys sharing his books with folk here in the valley."

As soon as the servant departed the room the lads attacked the stack of sandwiches. They were tasty morsels comprised of slabs of salty ham and slices of cheddar cheese on freshly baked, thickly sliced bread. The boys inhaled the sandwiches and apples and then drank the entire pot of tea, using every grain of the sweet sugar and every drop of the foamy cream.

They were just beginning to examine some of the books on the shelves when they heard movement and voices from elsewhere in the house. Soon they heard footfalls along the hallway outside the door to the study. Both boys turned and faced the door. Seconds later it opened and a handsome gentleman in riding clothes stepped into the room. He marched directly to the brothers, speaking as he walked.

"Good afternoon, lads," declared the man in a friendly voice. "Alfonso tells me that you are here to make an inquiry."

Justus took a step forward. "Yes, Mr. Bowie. First, please allow me to apologize for the intrusion. Circumstances did not allow us the opportunity to announce our coming. My name is Justus ..."

"I know exactly who you are," interrupted Mr. Bowie, smiling warmly. "You are Justus Avery. You are the very image of your father." He turned to Jonas. "And you must be Jonas." He shook both of their hands. "I have been expecting you, lads. I am so glad that you have finally come."

Justus and Jonas stood absolutely still, their mouths open wide in confusion and surprise.

Finally, Justus spoke. "You ... you *knew* we were coming?"

"Sooner or later. Your father believed so. He had great faith in his sons, and he was a very convincing man." Mr. Bowie's smile turned downward and converted into a sad frown. He motioned to a door that led outside to the garden. "Come, boys. There is something outside that you need to see."

14
PAPA'S SURPRISE

Justus and Jonas clutched their hats to their chests and wept as they stood over the grave. At the head of the oblong mound of earth was a lovely Christian cross. Clearly, it had been made by the hands of a skilled carpenter. Carved into the cross was the name Jeremiah Avery.

"Who made the cross?" asked Justus. "It is fine craftsmanship."

"Silas Philpot, one of our indentures. He is a master carpenter and was a good friend to your father. They worked together on occasion. It was his honor to make Jeremiah's grave marker. Indeed, he asked permission to do so."

"I shall have to thank him personally," declared Justus.

Justus, Jonas, and Mr. Bowie stared at the grave in reverent silence. After a short while, Mr. Bowie spoke softly.

"Jeremiah ached to see you boys. He held on for as long

as he could, but he was too weak and the fever that ravaged him was too strong. His body remained broken from all that he suffered in that horrible accident on board the ship. He never truly recovered from it. When the fever took hold there was nothing we could do for him."

"What manner of fever was it?" asked Jonas.

"We are not entirely certain, though one of the other workmen told me that he suffered the bite of a spider only days before he died. Of course, I summoned a physician to come and treat him, but by the time he arrived it was too late."

Justus wiped his tears on his sleeve. "This earth looks fresh. How long ago did he pass?"

"It's been three weeks now."

"We've been gone from Virginia just over two weeks," declared Jonas with a broken sob. "Papa died before we even fled the Dawson place ... before we even came to Maryland. We did all of this for nothing, Justus!" He buried his face into his brother's side and cried.

"No, it was not for nothing," Justus reassured him. "We went in search of our papa and now we have found him. We accomplished what we set out to do."

"But what will we do now? Where will we go?" moaned Jonas through his tears.

Justus wrapped his arm around his little brother's shoulder. "We will figure something out."

"Come, lads," interrupted Mr. Bowie. "Let us return to my study and talk."

Jonas turned to him. "After we talk, may I come back again and visit with Papa for a while longer?"

The man smiled warmly. "Of course. You may come to visit him any time that you wish."

Justus and Jonas returned their hats to their heads, nodded respectfully toward the grave, and then followed Mr. Bowie up the path that led back to the house.

One Hour Later

JUSTUS AND JONAS SAT ON A SMALL SOFA NEAR THE hearth. Mr. Bowie sat on the edge in a comfortable wing-back chair opposite them. Their tears had given way to laughter and joy. All three were laughing as Mr. Bowie recounted a rousing story about their father. He was waving his arms in the air as he attempted to help them visualize the scope of the event. It was a hilarious tale of a time when a goose, a bird destined for the Bowie family's dinner table, had escaped the grip of Mabel, the plantation's exceedingly large cook.

"I was in this very room when I heard a terrible commotion outside. I darted to the window just in time to see Mabel and your father running circles around that runaway bird. Mabel weighs every bit of three hundred pounds, so, needless to say, she was not moving very fast. And your father, God rest his soul, could barely walk to begin with due to his injured legs. But there he was, hot on the trail of Mabel and that cursed bird."

Justus laughed out loud. "Our father actually gave chase to the goose?"

"He certainly did! All three ran in perfect circles around the edge of the fenced garden, like it was a great race! The goose was in the lead, followed by Mabel. Your father was bringing up the rear, of course. The animal was honking and jumping about and attempting to fly. There were clouds of dust and feathers. Mabel was screaming and cursing the bird. Your father was laughing hysterically. And, of course, they were all three drawing quite a crowd of spectators. Two dozen servants and slaves surrounded the yard, all of them howling with laughter, yelling, and cheering. It was a grand spectacle, I promise you."

"Did the goose get away?" asked Jonas, giggling.

Mr. Bowie grinned. "Almost. But then suddenly, in the midst of the chase, the goose spotted an opportunity. It peeled away from the circle that they had all been running and then darted toward the open gate. He was but a few feet away from freedom. Just when it appeared the bird was going to escape with its life, your father performed one of the most amazing feats of athleticism that I have ever seen with my own eyes. From all the way across the lawn he launched one of his crutches at it!"

"Really?" exclaimed Jonas. "He tossed his crutch at the goose?"

Mr. Bowie shook his head. "He did simply not toss it. He launched it like an Indian throwing a spear. The thing flew through the air like a missile, absolutely straight as an arrow and at least thirty feet airborne. The tip of it struck the unsuspecting bird squarely in the back of the head. That goose dropped like a rock, dead before it hit the ground." He sighed happily and slapped his knee. "It was a perfect shot. I still do not understand how he did it."

"So, then, I take it that you and your family enjoyed goose for your supper that night?" asked Justus.

Mr. Bowie nodded and grinned. "We did, thanks to your father." He sighed happily. "That was when I first got to know him. My wife witnessed the spectacle, as well. She requested that, since he had saved our supper that night, we should invite him to join us. Of course, it is most inappropriate for a master to entertain one of his servants at a family meal. Still, she insisted. So, as in all things, I granted her request and invited your father to sup with us. I am most glad that I did."

"Why so?" asked Justus, intrigued.

"Because I discovered what a fine and honorable man your father was. During the course of our meal, thanks to my wife's amazing powers of interrogation, we learned your father's story of coming to America. He told us about your mother's death, about being injured while a substitute crewman, and then becoming separated from you. He told us about his indebtedness to the hospital and being sold into servitude. He shared everything with us. He even told us about the clue he left in the trunk back in Baltimore. He was absolutely convinced that, one day, you would follow his trail and come looking for him. And now here you are." He sat back in his chair and eyed the boys admirably. "And I must confess that I am most impressed. It was no small task to locate your father. His journey to this place, as well as yours, was a complicated one."

"Indeed, it was," agreed Jonas. "Was our father happy here?"

"As happy as one can be as an indentured servant, I suppose," replied Mr. Bowie honestly. "Of course, I regarded him differently after hearing his incredible story. He did not deserve what had happened to him, any more than you lads deserved the way that you were treated. I provided him with his own private quarters. He continued his work for me, of course. His cobblery was invaluable to our labors here. He kept all of my workers in serviceable shoes. I made sure that he was well-clothed and fed. And I entertained him here in this study from time to time. We occasionally shared a pipe and a brandy. I know it may sound a bit absurd, my being the master of this estate and he one of my servants ... but I am proud to say that I counted Jeremiah Avery as a friend." He sighed. "I truly miss him. All of us at *Willow* Creek do."

Justus and Jonas smiled as they pondered the man's kind words. Both were happy that their father had passed away in a place where he was loved and well-regarded.

"So, what will you boys do now? Where will you go?"

Justus shrugged and shook his head. "We do not know. We are, of course, runaways and fugitives. If we are caught, then we will be sent back to our master." He cut his eyes at Mr. Bowie. "Do you intend to hand us over?"

"No, Son. I would never do such a dishonorable thing. Unfortunately, I cannot harbor you here for any significant length of time. To do so would be unlawful. You may remain a day or two, and in the meantime, I will be honored to help you in any way that I can. I will write letters on your behalf and appeal to the authorities. I might even appeal to the governor. However, such efforts will require some time. Eventually, though, you will need to find another place to hide." He sighed thoughtfully. "Tell me, are your pursuers close by?"

"We hope not. One of our friends in Upper Marlborough, a young fellow named Craig MacLellan, was attempting to lead them astray. We do not know if he was successful."

"Well, let us pray that he was," declared Mr. Bowie,

standing. "That would buy us a little time to strategize. But, for now, let us go to your father's cottage. It has remained empty since he passed. His things are there. He wanted me to give them to you."

Justus and Jonas stood. "We are most grateful, Mr. Bowie, for your kindness and hospitality."

He nodded. "It is my pleasure, indeed, to welcome the sons of Jeremiah Avery. Now, come ... let us go to the cottage."

JUSTUS AND JONAS STOOD SIDE-BY-SIDE INSIDE THEIR father's tiny one-room house. It was sparsely furnished. There was a bed, a table and chair, and a washstand with a pitcher and bowl. A single plate, cup, fork, and spoon were arranged neatly on the tiny table, which sat near the stone hearth. Both boys stared mournfully at the bed where their father had slept each night. Nearby a stained linen shirt and a pair of wool breeches hung on nails driven into the wall. In the far corner, in front of a large window, was a workman's bench with an iron shoe mold mounted atop a thick hickory post. Beside the bench sat a long wooden box with a handle on top. The box was filled to overflowing with their father's shoe repair tools.

"Papa lived right here in this room," Jonas whispered in awe. "Just imagine that."

"And he died here," added Justus, his voice filled with sadness.

"He also worked here. He spent most of his time here in this cottage because of his disability. I required that all workers bring their shoes and leather work to him. It was both his home as well as his workspace. He enjoyed working over yonder in the light of the window. As you can see, your father lived the life of a simple man, but I believe he was content here," promised Mr. Bowie.

Justus turned and faced the gentleman. He asked him bluntly, "Did our father ever make mention of a treasure?"

"A *treasure*?" echoed Mr. Bowie in a disbelieving tone. He chuckled uncomfortably. "Whatever do you mean?"

Jonas explained, "There is talk of our father being in possession of a treasure. We heard our master's foreman mention it. According to him, Mr. Dawson is aware of it, as well as the man who sold us into servitude, Captain Ichabod Rochelle. It is the reason that Mr. Dawson has pursued us so relentlessly. According to the foreman, both Mr. Dawson and Captain Rochelle figured that we might lead them to our father and, thus, to the treasure. They were conspiring together to steal our father's money."

Mr. Bowie scoffed at the notion. He shook his head vehemently. "You are actually claiming that Benedict Dawson is part of a conspiracy that involves you, your father, a renegade ship's captain, and a missing treasure?"

Justus nodded. "Yes, sir. We heard with our own ears Mr. Dawson's foreman, Abram Sledge, attest to that set of facts."

"But what you are saying is utterly absurd for any number of reasons!" protested Mr. Bowie. "First, let me assure you that your father possessed no money at all. If he did, then why on earth would he have subjected himself to becoming an indentured servant? Furthermore, why would he remain one? Why would he not have purchased his own freedom? And I positively reject the notion that Benedict Dawson could be part of such a conspiracy. I know Benedict personally. He is a good friend, and he is, above all things, a gentleman."

"And yet he purchased us, at the time two helpless little boys, even though we swore to him that we were not orphans. He threatened us with punishment when we tried to explain to him what had happened to us and where our father had gone. He locked us away and worked us as slaves. And when we escaped his plantation, he sent forth his foreman with a pack of hounds to pursue us," retorted Jonas boldly. "His man even took a shot at us in Baltimore. Tell me, Mr. Bowie, are those the actions of a true gentleman?"

Mr. Bowie's face paled with shock. "You never mentioned hounds or gunplay." He looked at Justus. "Is this true?"

Justus nodded. "He sent an army of hired men and dogs after us all the way to Baltimore and back. They have been after us for over three weeks now."

"But ... but why?" stammered Mr. Bowie. "Why would Benedict Dawson pursue two runaway boys so diligently? Your indentures could not have been that expensive or valuable. It makes absolutely no sense."

"We believe it is because this rumor of a treasure is true," explained Justus. "Or at least it has a measure of truth to it. We know that our father brought his life savings with him on the journey to America, and we also know that the money disappeared. It was not inside his trunk that we discovered in his old shop in Baltimore. We know not what became of it. We assume that he must have carried it on his person."

"But if your father had a monetary savings, then why

did he not pay his debt when he was released from the hospital?"

Justus explained, "Because he lost all of his memory when he fell from the ship's mast. He did not only break his legs. He suffered a horrible blow to his head."

Mr. Bowie shook his head, still unconvinced. "But I know for a fact that your father recovered all of his memories. He told me about his life in England and all about you, his family, in vivid detail. Surely, he would also have recalled the whereabouts of his hidden savings. Why would he not then take his money and purchase his freedom?"

"Because he was saving it all for us," declared Jonas. "He was saving it to buy us land and a future. That is what *we* believe, at least."

"Also, he did not know who he could trust," added Justus. "Just imagine what might have happened to him, an indentured servant, if he suddenly produced some gold coins to pay off his own indenture. Surely, he would have been accused of thievery and locked away in jail. His master would have then claimed all his silver and gold. Everything he had would have been taken from him." Justus frowned. "The law is not kind to indentured folk, Mr. Bowie."

The man considered their words carefully. Still, he shook his head. "I simply cannot believe it. This tale is entirely too grand and outlandish to believe." He pointed to the box of tools in the corner. "Those cobblery tools were your father's only possessions. He brought them with him when I purchased his indenture. There was nothing else. There was no money."

"May we look at Papa's tools?" asked Justus.

"Of course. They belong to you now."

The three of them walked over to the work area. Justus picked up the toolbox by its handle and then placed it on top of the work bench. He and Jonas removed the tools, one at a time, and spread them across the bench. There were all manner of blades, awls, needles, and stamps. In the very bottom of the box Jonas found his father's cobbling hammer. He picked up the hammer and reverently cradled it in his hand. The ancient tool brought back a flood of memories as he recalled seeing his father using it on his workbench back in England.

"I remember this hammer," Jonas declared in a shaky voice. "Papa said that it was his grandfather's. He cherished it. Do you remember when Mother tried to get him to purchase a new one?"

Justus smiled. "I remember. But he absolutely refused. It was his great-grandfather's hammer. That tool is a family heirloom." He paused. "Perhaps the only family heirloom we have left."

Justus pointed to a brass cap that was tacked onto the end of the handle. It covered the entire end. The plate had the letter "A" on it alongside a tiny image of a cobbler's hammer. It was the mark that he placed on the soles of the shoes he repaired and was identical to the mark that they had found inside the trunk back in Baltimore.

"Look at how Papa put his special mark on it," he said. "He was *that* proud of it."

Mr. Bowie smiled and nodded. "Your father took great pride in his handiwork. He placed that mark upon every shoe or leather piece upon which he worked."

Jonas made a curious face. "It is odd, though, Justus. I don't remember that end plate or mark being there before." He weighed the hammer in his hand, bouncing it up and down, and then glanced at his brother. "And does this hammer seem unusually heavy to you?"

Justus took the hammer from his brother and balanced it in his hand. "Yes. That is so strange. It is *very* heavy." Suddenly, a look of realization and wonder filled his face. He exclaimed, "That's it. Jonas!"

"What's it?" asked his brother, confused.

Justus lay the hammer on the bench and quickly reached into his pocket. He removed the letter that their father had hidden for them inside the trunk and unfolded it.

"Who wrote that?" asked Mr. Bowie, intensely curious.

"Papa did," answered Justus. "We found it in a hidden compartment in his trunk. And it contains this mysterious riddle." He read the verse:

"Once in hand, ye sons of man, trusty tool of timber and steel;
Weigh carefully, lads, lest ye strike, a secret to reveal."

Jonas stared at the hammer. Suddenly, the riddle made complete sense to him. He exclaimed, "This hammer is papa's trusty tool of timber and steel!"

Justus nodded. "And we just weighed it and found it to be a bit too heavy."

"But what and where is the secret to be revealed?" asked Jonas.

Justus picked up the hammer and turned it upside down to examine the brass plate. It was held in place by three tiny nails, each one driven into the wood of the handle.

"Could it truly be that simple?" mumbled Justus.

"Could what be that simple?" demanded Jonas, completely confused. "Tell me, Brother!"

Justus ignored him. Quickly, he reached for a set of pliers and then carefully extracted the nails that held the brass cap in place. Once the nails were out, he removed the cap. He smiled when he saw a perfectly round hole, a half-inch wide, drilled into the end of the handle. There was a tiny wad of leather stuffed into the hole. He removed the leather plug and then inverted the hammer over the bench top. When he did so a perfect stack of shiny gold discs poured forth from the hole and scattered across the work bench.

"It is gold!" shouted Jonas. "We have found Papa's money!"

Mr. Bowie marveled at the pile of gold coins. "There must be fifty of them, all Spanish coins from Mexico City."

"What is their value?" asked Jonas.

Mr. Bowie grinned. "Four Spanish dollars each. That is over two hundred dollars in cash money."

Suddenly, Justus noticed a similar brass plated mounted on the side of the hickory post that held their father's iron shoe mold. It was positioned at the very bottom of the post. It bore the same mark, but it was square instead of round.

"Look!" he exclaimed. "That post has a plate on it, too!"

"Take it off!" urged Jonas. "There could be more!"

Justus quickly removed the four small nails that held the plate in place. When he pulled the last nail from the wood the brass plate fell away, and a wave of Spanish silver dollars poured out of the opening. As Justus moved them aside more and more coins came out. Soon there was a large pile of silver atop the work bench next to the gold.

"How many are there?" asked Jonas excitedly.

Justus counted them quickly. "Fifty-three."

Mr. Bowie shook his head, wide-eyed. "Good heavens! Your father *did* possess a great treasure!" He patted them on their shoulders. "And now all of this silver and gold is all yours."

15
FREEDOM AND LIBERTY

Two Weeks Later - May 1, 1775
Frederick County, Virginia

"Your proposal is preposterous, as is this entire meeting!" protested Benedict Dawson. He pointed angrily at the two gold coins lying on his desk. "I paid five times that amount for those boys when I purchased their indentures! I will not accept such a paltry sum in exchange for their release from service." He narrowed his eyes accusingly. "You have found the treasure, no doubt. How else would these miserable little paupers be wearing such expensive finery?"

The red-faced, frustrated, embarrassed man glared angrily at Justus and Jonas. The boys were seated across the desk from their master. They were, indeed, dressed as gentlemen, each of them clad in new suits. Justus wore a suit of indigo blue linen. Jonas' outfit was a rich, chocolatey brown. Their white linen shirts had fancy ruffles and they wore silver links on their cuffs. Each lad balanced a crisp, new felt tricorn on his knee. They did not at all look like indentured servants.

"I would say that you more than got your money's worth out of us, Mr. Dawson," retorted Justus. "We gave you five years of hard labor, both of us working like grown men."

"And what is this ridiculous talk of treasure?" mocked Walter Bowie, raising an eyebrow in feigned confusion. "What treasure must we have found?"

"Avery's treasure, of course!" barked Dawson.

"Jeremiah Avery was but a humble cobbler who suffered greatly from his injuries, and he was but a servant, himself," retorted Mr. Bowie. "How could he possess any manner of treasure?" He rose from his chair and then leaned forward, resting his knuckles on the desk, and inching close to his old friend. He hissed threateningly, "You *will* accept this deal, Benedict. You *will* grant their release and give me papers granting their freedom."

"And if I refuse?" questioned Mr. Dawson indignantly, crossing his arms.

"If you refuse then I will be compelled to inform the Royal Governor of Virginia, Lord Dunmore, of your illegal dealings with the nefarious Captain Ichabod Rochelle. I will tell him all about your relationship with that heinous crook of a Frenchman." He leaned even closer. Their noses almost touched. "How do you think the King's governor will feel about your having kidnapped English subjects into indentured servitude, and in collaboration with an outlaw Frenchman, no less?" He shook his head solemnly. "I rather think he would unleash an army of his tax men upon your plantation to pore over all of your financial records. I predict the jailhouse may be in your future, sir.

Surely you would not desire such an unfortunate and potentially ruinous series of events."

Mr. Dawson's face flushed crimson. The muscles in his cheeks quivered and flexed as he ground his teeth in anger and frustration.

"The choice is yours, Benedict. It is a simple one, really," declared Mr. Bowie, standing upright. He placed two documents in front of Dawson. "You may take this gold as payment in full and then sign these papers, or I can return at the end of the week with Lord Dunmore's tax examiners." He paused. "Oh, and by the way, your man, Abram Sledge, and his associate were apprehended by Maryland officials yesterday. During questioning they confessed to everything. They admitted knowing that the Avery boys were, indeed, free Englishmen. They admitted to your longstanding collusion with Ichabod Rochelle and the conspiracy to impress free folk into servitude. And they admitted your wanton pursuit of these boys and their father in order to steal away his life savings."

"You cannot prove any of it!" argued Mr. Dawson.

"I do not have to. The authorities in Maryland are already convinced by Mr. Sledge's sworn testimony. No doubt they will soon be in contact with their counterparts here in Virginia. The jig is up, Benedict. You have been found out. Now, either grant these boys their freedom or suffer the consequences of your illegal and ungentlemanly actions. Simply sign these papers and we will make it all go away."

With a flash of drama, he picked up the turkey feather quill from its stand, dipped it in the inkwell, and then held it in front of Dawson.

Mr. Bowie sneered. "Well? What will it be, Benedict, old friend?"

Benedict Dawson let loose a frustrated sigh of defeat. He snatched the quill from Mr. Bowie's hand and then hurriedly scribbled his signature on one paper, then dipped the quill once more and signed the other. Once done he angrily tossed both papers into Walter Bowie's face. They fell into the floor beside his feet.

"There you go, Walter. Now get out of this house! You are no longer a friend of mine. Never come back."

Mr. Bowie bent down and picked up the boys' freedom papers. He rolled them into the form of a tube and then lifted them to his forehead in a mocked salute.

"You are no gentleman, Benedict, and likely never have been. I will be sure to share that bit of information with everyone I know. Best of luck finding business partners in the future."

Mr. Dawson jumped to his feet and flashed an angry finger toward the door. "Get out! Get out, now! Before I let loose the hounds on you all!"

Mr. Bowie chuckled mockingly. "From what I hear they would likely not be able to find us even if our pockets were filled with fresh mutton." He glanced victoriously at the Avery boys. "Let's go, lads. We must shake the dust of this place from our shoes as quickly as possible."

He picked up his hat and tucked it beneath his arm. Without another word to the master of the plantation they marched from the room and closed the door closed behind them.

"I should say that went rather well," announced Mr. Bowie once they were outside. He handed the lads their papers. "You fellows are free men, and well-propertied, to boot. What will you do with yourselves now that you have your freedom and all that silver and gold?"

Justus looked at his brother. Jonas smiled happily and nodded.

"I sense another conspiracy brewing," announced Mr. Bowie, smiling. "What do you want?"

"If you do not mind, sir, we would appreciate a ride to Upper Marlborough. We have some business there, and we may need your adult assistance."

"What manner of business?" he asked, intrigued.

"We need to settle some taxes on a piece of land there. There is a house and a small piece of land that are obtainable through payment of back taxes."

Mr. Bowie nodded. "That is good thinking. Land and a home will be an excellent investment of your money."

"Well, it is not for us. It is for someone else. And we would also like purchase some indentures in the town."

"Two indentures, to be exact," added Jonas.

"You fellows fancy purchasing some personal servants for yourselves?" Mr. Bowie asked, somewhat in disbelief. "I should think you have had enough of servitude."

"No, sir," answered Justus. "But we do fancy setting two of our friends free."

"Of course, you do." Mr. Bowie sighed happily and nodded. "It will be my pleasure to assist. Whilst you pay off the land, I will draw up proper freedom papers for your friends."

They walked to Mr. Bowie's carriage. He and Jonas climbed aboard. As Justus stepped his foot onto the side rail, he noticed movement in one of the upper-floor windows of the Dawson house. A girl was standing there. It was Drusilla Dawson, the daughter of Benedict. She was the kindly girl who had taught both boys to read and then later aided them in their escape.

She waved to Justus and then flashed him a friendly smile. He smiled and waved back at her. She quickly turned and walked away from the window and out of view. Justus shrugged and then climbed into the carriage. Seconds later they were rolling northeastward toward the Potomac River.

Early Afternoon
The Sleeping Bear Tavern

"I DON'T KNOW, LAD," SAID JACOB SWEENEY, THE tavern owner. "Charity is a mighty fine servant girl. I'm not sure I want to let her go. She will be mighty hard to replace."

"There are plenty of young women hereabouts looking for honest work, Mr. Sweeney. Any would serve you for a decent wage." He sighed impatiently. "I do not wish for Charity MacLellan to be indentured another day. I have her papers ready for your signature. Name your price."

Sweeney placed both hands on the bar and stared at Justus with a steely gaze. "Very well, then. How about ten dollars?"

"Done!" declared Justus.

He reached into his coin purse and removed five tiny gold coins. He placed them side-by-side on the counter. Mr. Sweeney stared at the gold, wide-eyed.

"Where did you get them coins?" he demanded, his voice shaky.

"That is none of your concern," responded Walter Bowie, stepping forward with a document, quill, and small inkwell. "Please sign here."

"But I cannot read or write," confessed the man.

"Then make your mark. I will witness it."

The tavern keeper took the paper and feather in hand. He dipped the nib into the ink bottle and then scratched a ragged "X" on the document. Mr. Bowie then added the words, "Witnessed By," and signed his own name. He blew on the ink to ensure it was dry.

"That concludes our business," said Justus. "Where is Charity now?"

"She went over to the livery just a little while ago to take dinner to her cousin. I expect her back any time."

"You should not expect her back at all, Mr. Sweeney," Justus corrected him, waving his finger. "You are no longer her employer."

Justus, Jonas, and Mr. Bowie turned and walked toward the door. Sweeney called to them as Jonas lifted the latch.

"I would have taken two dollars for her, you know." He regarded them with a hateful sneer. "She's likely not even worth that. You got taken on that deal."

Justus turned proudly and retorted, "I would have given a hundred dollars for her freedom, Mr. Sweeney. So then, who truly got taken on the deal?" He placed his tricorn cocked hat on his head and then tipped it respectfully. "I will send someone for Charity's things straightaway. Good day to you, sir."

The surly, whisker-faced tavern keeper stared at them in wide-eyed disbelief as they exited his business and then closed the door.

❧

Two Hours Later

THE AVERY BROTHERS AND MR. BOWIE STRODE HAPPILY through the open doors of the livery stable. They did not see anyone inside the building, but they could hear voices.

Justus called out, "Hello! Has anyone seen two runaways? They are a handsome pair and look something like us."

Almost instantly a pair of heads appeared from behind the low wall of a nearby stall. It was Charity and her cousin, Craig MacLellan. The ever-hungry Craig was gnawing on a smoked turkey leg and grinning from ear to ear.

"You fellows have gone and interrupted my dinner," he teased.

"Justus! Jonas!" exclaimed Charity with glee.

She darted out of the stall and ran to them, tumbling into their waiting embraçe. Craig followed closely behind, still eating his turkey leg.

Charity babbled excitedly, bombarding them with questions and concerns. "But ... but I do not understand. Why are you here? Why are you dressed so strangely? Those men and their dogs are surely still after you! Aren't you afraid?"

Jonas shook his head. "Calm down, Charity. No one is after us. We are free and have the documents to prove it." He smiled and motioned toward the gentleman accompanying them. "This is Mr. Walter Bowie. He has been a tremendous help to us."

Mr. Bowie nodded to Charity. "Miss MacLellan, I am

pleased to finally make your acquaintance. These intrepid lads have told me much about you." He winked at Craig. "And your exploits are legendary, Mr. MacLellan."

Craig's expression was blank. He professed, "I don't know what that means, sir."

Everyone but Craig laughed uproariously.

"But how did you accomplish it all?" asked Charity once the laughter died down. "Did Mr. Bowie purchase your indentures and set you free?"

"No," Mr. Bowie clarified, shaking his head. "All I did was draft all the legal papers. Justus and Jonas purchased their own freedom."

Craig instantly stopped chewing on his turkey leg. He exclaimed, grease dribbling down his skinny chin, "Then you boys did it! You found your father and his treasure!"

Jonas nodded solemnly, his proud smile morphing into a frown. A tear leaked from one of his eyes. "Yes, we found him."

Charity took the boy's hand. "But what is wrong, Jonas? You should be thrilled. Wasn't your father happy to see you?"

Justus explained, "Papa died a few weeks before we arrived at Mr. Bowie's plantation. He suffered a terrible fever and then passed."

"Oh, Justus! Oh, Jonas! I am so sorry," said Charity, her lip quivering. She squeezed both boys' hands reassuringly. "I know that both of you loved him so."

"Yes. That we did," declared Justus. "And he loved us back. He provided for us well. We did, indeed, find his life savings ... what those men pursuing us had been calling his 'treasure.' Now we intend to put it, along with our newly purchased liberty, to some good use."

"How so?" she asked, intrigued.

Justus explained, "We have been talking things over with Mr. Bowie these past couple of weeks. He believes that our efforts and money would be wasted if we went into land and farming. He has helped us realize that we possess some unique skills when it comes to finding people and things. We apparently proved that through our quest to locate our father." He looked at Mr. Bowie. "What was that word you used to describe us?"

"Tenacious," answered Mr. Bowie, smiling. Noting the look of confusion on Craig's face, he explained, "That means 'hard-headed, Mr. MacLellan.'"

"Oh," acknowledged Craig, nodding his head. Everyone laughed again.

Justus continued, "Mr Bowie believes that we could utilize our tenacious skills to make a living for ourselves."

"I do not understand," Charity confessed. "How? You are both so young."

Mr. Bowie stepped forward. "With my recommendation and backing, Justus and Jonas are going to open a new business. They are going to put their talents and skills to use as private investigators."

"Private investigators?" echoed Craig. "What are they?"

"They are individuals who find missing people, locate lost things, solve mysteries, and assist law enforcement in solving crimes and apprehending criminals," explained Mr. Bowie. "Justus and Jonas have proven themselves very good at finding things and solving mysteries. The search for their father included making hundreds of inquiries, interviewing folk, searching for public records, and finding hidden clues." He winked at Jonas. "They even stretched the law a bit and snuck into a hospital in the dead of night.

To be certain, they are excellent investigators. And as there are very few such skilled individuals working privately in these Colonies, I daresay there will be many needy folks in search of their skills."

"And you think people will actually *pay* them to do those sort of things?" asked Craig, his voice filled with doubt.

"Most certainly," Mr. Bowie assured him. "It may take some time to solve a few more mysteries and establish a reputation in the Maryland colony, but I have no doubt at all that theirs will be a thriving business. I am so confident, in fact, that I have agreed to be a financial partner in the endeavor."

"Where will you operate this new business?" asked Charity shyly.

"Right here ... in Upper Marlborough," Jonas answered. "We intend to call this village our home. We have already paid the first month's rent for a small storefront here in town. It has space for an office below and ample living quarters above for Justus and me."

Charity clapped her hands together. "Oh, that is positively wonderful! You will be just down the street from the tavern. I shall serve and fetch your meals every day."

"About that ..." Justus interrupted her. "You don't work at the *Sleeping Bear* anymore. And you are no longer indentured to Sweeney. We have purchased out your indenture. You are free." He nodded to Mr. Bowie. "Here are your papers."

Mr. Bowie handed her a document. Charity remained utterly silent as she received it. Her eyes, already red and swelled, overflowed with tears of joy as she read the words.

"I ... I do not know what to say. Am I truly free from servitude?"

Jonas took her hand. "Yes, you are. And you don't have to say anything at all. It is our joy and honor to give you this gift. After all, you have done so much for us."

She wept tears of joy. "But where will I go now? I lived in that cursed old tavern for years now. I have no other place to go."

"Yes, you do. You will go home, of course," Justus answered her, a smile filling his face. He nodded again to Mr. Bowie.

The gentleman handed her another document. "Miss MacLellan, Justus and Jonas Avery have paid the pending taxes on your deceased parents' land and have obtained a deed for the house, along with fifteen acres of surrounding fields and woodlands. That deed is in *your* name."

She trembled with emotion. "You mean ... you mean ... the house is *truly* mine?"

"Completely yours," Justus assured her. "And we pre-paid the taxes for the next three years. That should be enough time for you to turn a profit from the land, or start a business, or do whatever else your heart desires. You can even go back to work at the tavern, if doing so pleases you."

"Not likely!" she retorted.

Again, another chorus of laughter ensued.

"That there is a mighty noble thing for you boys to do," acknowledged Craig, his own voice cracking with emotion. "You have blessed Charity beyond measure."

Justus cut a sly grin at his brother and Mr. Bowie. "Well, as it turns out, she's going to need a little help with that land. How about you to saddle that matching pair of sorrel mares from out back and then head on out to the house before sundown?"

"What?" asked Craig, thoroughly confused.

"Those horses are yours now," Mr. Bowie explained as he handed Craig a piece of paper. "Along with your freedom. The lads purchased your indenture, as well, and then promptly released you from service."

"We ran into the livery master down at the tavern," explained Justus. "He took a few coins and signed your papers. We got you for a bargain, actually." He winked.

"I ... I ... I can't think of anything to say!" Craig exclaimed happily.

"Now, there's a first," Jonas chided him as he rolled his eyes.

Again, the entire group burst forth in joyful laughter.

Justus turned to Charity. "Actually, the two of you need to go to the house as quickly as possible. We purchased two new beds, one for you and one for Craig, at the furniture store. They will be delivering them before sundown. They'll need your key to get in and set them up. We'll be out later to check on you." He nodded to Craig. "A plow and other farming tools will be delivered tomorrow."

Charity leapt into his arms, smothered him with a huge hug, and then kissed him soundly on the cheek. Sensing his awkward discomfort, she quickly broke away from the embrace. His face flushed bright red. She wiped the happy tears from her cheeks. "I thank you all. And I will be expecting you all for supper." She took Craig by the hand. "Come, Cousin, we have much work to do before our guests arrive."

Charity dragged Craig toward the horse pen. He was

still clutching his greasy turkey leg. The Avery brothers laughed happily as they watched them go.

"It is a fine thing that you fellows have done this day," said Mr. Bowie admiringly. "You know, up in Massachusetts a rebellion has started. There were recently battles at Lexington and at Concord. It is all over the newspapers. Men have taken up arms against King George. It seems they have a notion that we should all be free from the tyranny of England. It is a grand aim, I must admit. But is seems to me to be almost unattainable."

"Do you think America could ever really do something like that?" asked Jonas. "Could the Colonies become free from England? Can we become our own nation?"

The man shrugged. "I do not know for certain. But what I do know is that you boys have inspired me this day. I have witnessed you set four people free, including yourselves." He chuckled. "If you keep up this pace, sooner or later we may very well see this entire country set free." He looked admiringly at Justus and Jonas. "You are just a pair of liberty-minded lads, aren't you?"

Justus smiled. "Yes, sir, we are. And you just gave me a wonderful idea!"

EPILOGUE

One Week Later

The Avery brothers stood in front of their office with Charity by their side. Justus pointed proudly at the sign dangling from the front post. It read, *The Liberty Lads Investigations*.

"What do you think, Charity?"

She nodded. "I like it. But where did that name come from? Shouldn't it just be *Avery Brothers Investigations*?"

Justus shook his head. "Something Mr. Bowie said to us last week stuck with me. After we paid off all of our indentures, he told us that we were 'a pair of liberty-minded lads.' So, Jonas and I agreed that this should be the name and identity of our enterprise. We want to work to set people free from the mysteries, problems, and secrets that plague their lives. So, from this day on we shall be known as *The Liberty Lads*." He paused and then added. "We were actually hoping that you might come to work for us. We need someone to take care of the office, greet customers, and take messages and such. You would be a most able assistant and partner."

Charity stared at them incredulously. "You mean you need someone to sit here and mind the store while you two roam about the countryside enjoying all your mysteries and adventures?"

Jonas grinned. "Something like that. Though we will, no doubt, need the ideas and contributions of a lady from time to time." He patted her on the shoulder. "You did a pretty fair job on that one assignment at the Treadway estate. I think you have some talent for investigations."

"Only a fair job?" she retorted, her fists resting defiantly on her hips. "I'll have you know I did a fantastic job!"

"Yes, you did," confessed Justus. "So, then, will you come to work with us? We really do need you."

She nodded. "I can agree to such an arrangement, but I'll expect to be well-paid for my efforts and skills."

Justus chuckled. "I imagined as much. You will be generously compensated ... *if* we ever get paid."

She nodded. "Very well, then. I am in your employ. But what does that even look like right now? There is nothing for us to investigate. Now that you have solved ***The Secret of the Runaway Servants***, will you simply sit around the office and wait for your first customer to show up?"

Jonas shook his head. "By no means. *You* will remain at the office. We depart for Philadelphia first thing in the morning. We have to get right to work on our next mystery right away."

"Philadelphia?" she shrieked in disbelief. "And what mystery will you be attempting to solve there?"

"It is ***The Mystery of the Missing Brother***, of

course," Justus answered confidently. "And we fully intend to solve it."

"Whose brother is missing?"

Both boys smiled warmly at her. "Yours," Justus answered. "We intend to find your brother, Andrew MacLellan, for you. And we already have a clue indicating he spent some time in Philadelphia."

"Where did you come across such a clue?" she asked.

"From a trustworthy source," promised Justus, winking. "If not, then we would not be traveling so far from home."

She nodded. A single tear escaped her right eye and then tumbled down her cheek. "Very well, then. Let us get to work. We must prepare you for the long journey."

Arm-in-arm, the three friends entered the office of *The Liberty Lads Investigations*.

A MESSAGE FROM THE AUTHOR

I hope that you enjoyed this first book in ***The Liberty Lads Mystery Series***. It was a pleasure preparing and writing it for you. I am just a simple "part-time" author, and I am humbled that you chose to read my book.

I would humbly ask that you help me spread the word about my historical fiction books for kids. You can help me in a number of ways.

- **Tell your friends.** There is nothing like "word of mouth" to stir interest in a new book.
- **Mention my books on Facebook or in other social media.** I know lots of students use social media these days. Please mention me, or maybe even post a picture of you reading one of my books!
- **Get your parents to write a review for me on Amazon.com.** Reviews are so very important. They help other readers discover good books. Tell your parents what you thought

about the book and ask them to put your words into the review.

- **Ask your local library to carry my books.** Librarians love suggestions from their readers.
- **Connect with me and like my author page on Facebook @cockedhatpublishing, and follow me on Twitter @GeoffBaggett.**
- **Tell your teachers about me.** I have a unique and interesting Revolutionary War presentation available for elementary and middle school classes. I actually bring a trunk full of items from the American Revolution and provide a "hands-on" experience for students. I am a professional speaker and living historian, and I absolutely love to travel and visit in schools. Get your teachers to contact me through my web site, geoffbaggett.com, or through my Facebook author page, to arrange an event.

Thanks, again, for reading my story. Be sure to tell all of your friends about ***The Liberty Lads*** mystery series. Book two will be coming soon!

Geoff Baggett

ABOUT THE AUTHOR

Geoff Baggett is a historical researcher and author with a passion for all things Revolutionary War. He is an active member of the Sons of the American Revolution and the Descendants of Washington's Army at Valley Forge.

Geoff has discovered over twenty American Patriot ancestors in his family tree. He is an avid living historian, appearing regularly in period clothing and uniforms in classrooms, reenactments, and other commemorative events. He lives with his family on a quiet little place in the country in rural western Kentucky.

OTHER BOOKS FOR YOUNG READERS

BY GEOFF BAGGETT

Patriot Kids of the American Revolution Series

Book 1 - Little Hornet

Book 2 - Little Warrior

Book 3 - Little Spy of Vincennes

Book 4 - Little Brother

Book 5 - Little Camp Follower

Book 6 - Little Turncoat

Book 7 -Little Drummer

Kentucky Frontier Adventures

Book 1 - A Bucket Full of Courage

Book 2 - Always Looking For a Home

www.ingramcontent.com/pod-product-compliance
Lightning Source LLC
LaVergne TN
LVHW091142080826
845145LV00008B/2225

* 9 7 8 1 9 4 6 8 9 6 0 5 6 *